MISSING

MISSING

CATHERINE MACPHAIL

BLOOMSBURY

First published in Great Britain in 2000
Bloomsbury Publishing Plc, 38 Soho Square, London, W1V 5DF

Printed in Great Britain by Clays Ltd, St Ives plc

10 9 8 7 6 5 4 3

For Janice, with love.

CHAPTER ONE

POW! POW!
PZAM! BANG!
1,800 points! MIGHTY MAX IS NOW THE
CHAMPION!
DO YOU WISH TO CONTINUE OR
SURRENDER?

Surrender? The word wasn't in her vocabulary. She punched the machine to continue.

SPLAT! KERPOW! PZAM!
BANG! BANG! BANG! YOU ARE NOW
DEAD!

The 1,800 points disappeared from the screen. She was champion no more. Mighty Zola had won.

'Cheat!' she shouted at the musclebound figure, standing hands on hips, jeering at her from the screen.

She was suddenly angry at him. Angry at the world.

'Cheat!' she said again, louder this time. Others in the arcade stopped playing their machines to look up at her. Let them look, she thought. She'd give them something to see. She banged the screen with her fist. Lights began flashing all around the edges. She'd like to wipe that superior grin right off Mighty Zola's face. Smash it off! She lifted her rucksack and threw it at him.

'Cheat!' she screamed.

'What's going on down there?' A sudden yell came from the back of the arcade. Mr Simms, Simmy, leaned out of his booth. His eyes flashed when he caught sight of her. 'You!' He began to try to pull his great bulk from the tiny booth.

'I know you, Maxine Moody! If you've broken that machine, I'll have the police on you!' His great belly wobbled and jiggled as he struggled to free himself. Maxine stuck out her tongue at him. He trembled with anger. 'I'm coming!' he warned her.

'Christmas will be here sooner,' she shouted back, then she whooped with delight and raced from the arcade.

'I'm phoning the police!' His shout followed her onto the street. He wouldn't phone the police, though. Not

Simmy. He'd be the one in trouble because she was there in the first place. She was only thirteen. Under-age. She should be at school. Simmy knew that. What did he care? Her money was as good as anybody else's. The Mighty Zola was her best game. She was better than anybody at it. Highest Points Champion, except when Zola himself cheated and beat her. She skipped along the street, her good mood back defiantly. No wonder she was good. She'd had plenty of practice. She spent a lot of time at Simmy's arcade. Had done since ...

She pushed the thought from her mind. She wouldn't think about that now. It was too nice today.

Elated, she whirled about in the street, flinging her rucksack around her. It caught someone full in the stomach. They grabbed her bag and almost pulled her off her feet.

'Hey!' she shouted, still dizzy. 'What do you think –'

A face glared back at her. She knew him. Cam. In her school. Two years above her. A swot. A clever clogs. His father owned one of the local Chinese restaurants. She'd never seen Cam smiling once.

Well, she could glare as good as he could any day.

'You got a problem?' she asked.

'You missed school again,' he said stiffly.

'So clever of you to notice. No wonder you're top of the class.'

'You're a very stupid little girl.'

'Little girl! I'm thirteen!'

'With the brain of a five-year-old. Amazing.' Was he trying to be witty? She'd show him.

'At least I've got a brain.' Which was just about the stupidest thing she could say. Cam was on the school quiz team, and they always won the championship hands down because of him. She suddenly realised she couldn't stand him. She hardly knew him, but she couldn't stand him.

'Why do you do this?' he went on. 'Haven't your parents suffered enough?'

Now at least she had a reason to hate him. It was all she needed.

'Mr Perfect!' she yelled at him. 'Don't you ever do anything wrong?' She yanked her rucksack from him. 'You don't know anything!' And she began running away from him.

No one understood. No one ever had. No one cared. Not her parents. Not anyone.

Hadn't THEY suffered enough?

Well, hadn't she?

Ten months now Derek had been gone. Her big brother. He'd been the same age as she was now when, on a day like any other, he'd gone off to school and just never came back. Missing. Like so many others. Months of waiting and praying and doing everything possible to find him had resulted in nothing. Not a trace. Mum and Dad had even gone on national television to appeal for his return. He'd been getting into trouble at school, playing truant, fighting. Mum and Dad were always on his back about something, and that morning there had been another stupid quarrel. Maxine couldn't even remember what it had been about. But if he would just come back, everything would be all right, they assured him. All they wanted was his safe return.

But he didn't come back.

And as the months dragged on, hopes for his return began to fade. Sightings of him at bus stops, in parks and railway stations all led nowhere. Derek had disappeared into thin air.

Yet her parents never gave up hope. Never stopped trying. Derek became their whole life, all they thought about.

And that was when Maxine realised that her parents hadn't any room in their thoughts, in their hearts ... for her. Everything was Derek. When news of him came from London or Birmingham or Cornwall, she was packed off to her gran's or some neighbours while her parents followed up every sighting. Their holidays were spent tracing every clue which might lead them to their son, while Maxine was deposited with whoever could be bothered having her. It had taken her a long time, but the truth finally dawned on her.

They just didn't care about her.

Sometimes she would catch her mum looking at her strangely. It didn't take her long to figure out what that look was.

Her mother was thinking, Why couldn't it have been you?

Hadn't her parents suffered enough?

They at least had each other. She had nobody.

There were times she almost hated Derek. He was only a vague figure to her now. Sandy hair hanging over his forehead, a mischievous grin – that was as much as she could picture of him. And yet she hated him.

Sometimes she wished that he had just died.

Oh! She hadn't meant to think that. It was a sin! Yet it seemed to come to her mind so often these days.

She realised she was close to St Jude's, their local

church. She would go there and pray. It was the only place she ever found any comfort.

They'd be expecting her home. Well, let them wait. She could use popping into the church as her excuse. They couldn't fault her for that.

St Jude's it was. She looked up and down the street. Busy with shoppers, people coming and going. Not one of them looking her way, and yet ... She stood still for a moment.

Why did she always have the feeling someone was watching her?

CHAPTER TWO

The church was cool and quiet. The traffic passing outside could have been a million miles away.

Maxine lit a candle and pressed it into place. She looked up at the statue standing above her. St Anthony. He was supposed to find lost things, but she had been praying to him since her brother disappeared and he hadn't found Derek.

His look seemed to be accusing her. Maybe she hadn't prayed hard enough. Maybe he knew ... knew she didn't want Derek back? That she wanted the memory of him out of her life for ever. Gone.

Oh no! Why did she think terrible things like that? She came here to ask for forgiveness and here she was, sinning again.

'Hello, Maxine. Can I help you?'

Maxine turned round guiltily as if she'd been caught

with her hand in the poor box. Father Matthew stood in front of her. Young, red-haired and freckled, he always seemed to Maxine to have a permanent grin on his face. He was smiling now. 'Did you want anything?'

Silly question, she thought. What did he think she was here for? The weekly shopping?

'I was just going.'

She stood up. Father Matthew didn't move. Maxine felt as if he was barring her way. 'You come in here quite often ... during the week.'

Meaning, of course, she wasn't here on Sunday when she was supposed to be. Maxine always assured her mum and dad that she was simply going to a later mass, then spent her Sunday morning with the Mighty Zola.

Did Father Matthew know that? She had a feeling that he knew something.

'Have to go.' She began pushing past him. 'Mum worries if I'm late.'

Surely even he wouldn't be so thick as not to understand that. He actually blushed and stepped aside. 'Of course. Sorry.'

Her shoes clattered as she hurried up the tiled floor of the church. As she reached the door she turned to say goodbye to him. There he was, framed against the stained-glass window, his red hair glowing in the late afternoon sun. He looked almost like a saint himself.

Except for his eyes. They were watching her strangely. Just as her parents sometimes did. Was he trying to understand her too? Or could he see through her, see her for what she was? A sinner.

Her father was waiting for her in the hallway when she returned home. 'Where have you been?' he asked grimly.

She put on her most saintly expression. 'I've been to church.'

A look of hurt passed over his face. 'You little liar,' he said through his teeth.

That hurt. She shouted back, 'It's true, actually. Ask Father Matthew.'

'You went there then ... after school?'

As he spoke he was pushing open the living-room door.

'Yes, I ...' Uh-oh. The first face she saw, even before her mother's tear-stained one, was that of Miss Ross, her class teacher.

They knew.

Miss Ross stood up. They called her Smiler at school.

16

She always looked so happy, with her short, glossy hair that shimmered whenever she laughed. However, she wasn't laughing now. She was growling. Growling at Maxine.

'Did you really think you could get away with it, Maxine?' she asked. Her voice was cold. It wasn't usually like that. Usually Maxine could talk to Miss Ross. She understood how she felt. Tried to, anyway. 'You promised me you'd come to school every day.'

Her mother's eyes filled with tears. 'You promised me too!'

She didn't want to hurt her mum. She wanted, right at that moment, to run to her. In a second she might have done it.

'Do you know what we thought when you didn't come home?' Her father's voice was angry. 'Do you know what your mother thought?'

Her mother crumpled into a chair, her face in her hands.

'Now you see what you've done!' Her dad sat down beside Mum, arms around her, comforting her.

Her mum looked up at her, drawing back a sob. 'It was just like Derek. Can't you see that, Maxine? You went to school, or so we thought, and then we found out you didn't. Just like ... just like ...'

Just like Derek. Why did everything always have to come back to Derek? He was never out of the conversation for long, nor out of anyone's thoughts. No matter what she did to get their attention, it always came back to Derek.

She might as well not exist.

'Where were you?' her dad demanded.

Maxine only shrugged.

'This has got to stop!'

She stared at him defiantly. She shouldn't. She knew that. There was a time when she wouldn't have dared. Would never have wanted to. But what did it matter now? What did it matter what she did? They didn't love her. They loved Derek. Always would.

CHAPTER THREE

'Are you all right?' Miss Ross said.

Maxine had been sent to her room in disgrace as usual. Miss Ross had knocked gently at her door and found Maxine sitting straight-backed on the window seat, staring outside.

What had she expected to find? Maxine with her face down on the bed, in floods of tears? Not Maxine Moody! She didn't answer and Miss Ross took her silence as an accusation. 'I didn't betray you,' she went on in a rush. 'I had to tell your parents you weren't at school. They worry about you.'

Maxine shrugged. 'I don't care.'

Miss Ross sat beside her on the window seat. 'You're not making things any better behaving like this. You're hurting them. You're hurting yourself.'

Maxine shrugged again.

'They're afraid the same thing might happen to you.'

Sometimes she could confide in Miss Ross. Tell her little things. Miss Ross had never known Derek. She'd come to the school only after he disappeared, so she wasn't one of the teachers who said that Maxine wasn't the clever pupil her brother was, or that she was almost as much trouble as he had been at the end. Miss Ross only knew Maxine, and seemed to like her. 'They keep hoping he'll come back,' Maxine said.

'That's only natural. Maybe he will.'

The thought appalled Maxine. Derek back? She couldn't picture him any longer. His face was a blur, though photographs of him were dotted everywhere about the house.

But Derek back? She knew she didn't want that. She wanted him wiped out of her life, all their lives, for ever. The way you erase a file on a computer or a tape on a video machine. If only getting rid of Derek was as easy as that.

She never wanted him back.

If he came back ... there would be no room for her at all. She would be shoved out, completely forgotten. No. Derek couldn't come back. Why couldn't he just be *dead*?

She gasped as she thought it, and Miss Ross glanced at her.

'What's wrong, Maxine?' She waited for an answer. She always wanted Maxine to tell her more, to confide in her. 'Confession is good for the soul,' she would say, like Father Matthew. But how could she tell her what she'd been thinking? How could she tell anyone that? She was a monster.

Suddenly she wanted Miss Ross away. She wanted to be alone so she could cry or scream, do whatever she wanted.

Miss Ross sensed her withdrawal and stood up to go. 'I'm on your side, Maxine. Please remember that. I might have to tell your parents when you don't come to school, but I am your friend. Please believe that.'

Maxine smiled. Her friend. Over the last year, Maxine had lost all her friends. Their sympathy had turned to annoyance at her behaviour. She was glad of Miss Ross. Since she'd come to the school, she had been the only one to try to understand. Maxine couldn't risk losing her. 'Thank you, Miss Ross. I am grateful. Honest.'

Miss Ross touched her hair gently. 'I'm always here for you to talk to.'

'I'll try harder,' Maxine promised.

Over the next few weeks, she did try. She didn't miss a day at school. All the teachers had instructions anyway to tell on her if she did. She tried not to let it bother her when her parents shut the door on her to share their own private grief. She tried to be a model daughter. And did they appreciate it? Not likely. Her mother didn't seem to care, and her father was only watching and waiting for her to step out of line again.

And school was no fun anyway. Sweeney was up to his old tricks – the most vicious boy Maxine had ever come across. Everyone in the school was either afraid of him or sensible enough to be wary of him. It was wise to keep out of Sweeney's line of vision, or else he might just notice you and make your life hell.

For the moment Sweeney's attention was taken up with a boy in Maxine's class, Paul Wilson. He had been chosen months ago as the awful Sweeney's new victim.

Once it had been Derek. When Derek first went to the high school, he had been so looking forward to it. Then Sweeney had come into his life and everything had changed. Sweeney with his meanness and his cruelty. Maxine could remember that time still, and the pain it caused. Derek hurrying home with disgusting spit all over his face and hair. Derek with dog's dirt emptied into his rucksack and all his school books covered in it. Derek bruised and bleeding after being chased and caught by Sweeney and his cronies. It seemed Mum and Dad spent half their lives in the headmaster's office complaining. And did it do them any good? Not likely. Sweeney always got off lightly. 'A poor boy, from a deprived background. We have to make allowances,' the headmaster would say. And Sweeney would be suspended for a few days, but then he would be back, back with a vengeance, and life for Derek grew even worse. The real problem was that Sweeney's family were as bad as he was. Never out of trouble, they thought being a 'man' meant hurting people and humiliating them and making them suffer.

'Fight back!' her dad would tell Derek. But how do you fight back against someone who always has at least six to back him up? Sweeney didn't fight fair. He liked his victims to be held down while he pummelled them. But eventually Derek had fought back. Only he hadn't fought Sweeney. Instead, he fought just about everyone else in the school. And that was when he started getting into trouble.

'I see,' Dad would say. 'Now you're the one that's the bully.'

And Derek would snap back, 'Bullies seem to be better treated. Why not!'

Trouble added to more trouble, until finally Derek ran away. And it had all begun with Sweeney. Maxine hated him. Everyone in school did. But nothing was ever done about him. Now they all watched helplessly as Paul Wilson's life was made a living hell by him.

We should be able to do something! Maxine thought as she watched one day as Sweeney forced Paul to hand over all the money in his pockets. Even that didn't satisfy Sweeney. He'd replace it, he said, so no one could say he was stealing, then Maxine and half the school watched in horror as he rasped phlegm from the bottom of his throat, held open Paul's pocket and and grogged it inside.

Sweeney guffawed with laughter. 'And there's plenty more where that came from, Paulyboy. I've got an unlimited supply!'

Paul just stood there, humiliated, red-faced and help-less. What was the point of going to a teacher? What would Sweeney's punishment be, if any? A reprimand or a few days' suspension. And then he would be back. And Paul knew what that would mean. So he stood there, his head hanging low, doing nothing.

As Sweeney was passing her, Maxine couldn't keep her mouth shut. 'You're disgusting!'

'Oh, listen to this, boys!' He beckoned to his mates. 'Maxine Moody has a mouth. And it's too big if you ask me.'

'One day you're going to be sorry, Sweeney. Somebody's going to get their own back on you.'

He stood before her, a tall boy, broad, his mouth always curled into a sneer.

'Well, it's not going to be your wimp of a brother, is it?'

He sniggered as he walked away and Maxine angrily shouted after him, 'He'll come back one day ... and he'll get you!'

That only made him laugh even louder. She was ready to run after him, no matter how many of his so-called friends were with him. Run and kick him and ... suddenly, she was grabbed by the jacket and held back.

'You *have* got a big mouth!' It was Cam, shaking his head in disbelief. 'Do you want him to start on you?'

'I'm only a girl. I'm not worth bothering about.'

'There's always a first time,' Cam warned her. 'Why are you so angry?'

'Because I hate Sweeney! I hate this school! I hate my life!' And she pulled away from him and ran.

And she did hate her life. No matter what she did, it was always the wrong thing.

'Miracles will never cease,' her father said one morning at breakfast. 'Three weeks at school and not a day off. Goodness! What did we do to deserve this?'

He was waiting to take Mum to her job in a local solicitor's office. 'Leave it, Jim,' her mother said. 'Just leave it be.'

Her mother didn't even want to talk about it.

Maxine watched as her mother stood up and took the breakfast dishes to the sink.

Her father was already at the front door. 'Make sure you get to school today. Why spoil the habit of three weeks?'

Her mother gave her a small wave as she left, just a fleeting gesture with her hand. Hardly worth the bother really.

Her real attention, her real goodbye, was for the photograph on the hall table. Derek, taken on his thirteenth birthday, just weeks before he disappeared. Maxine could remember the day well. For once, her bad-tempered, moody brother had been happy. She had saved up for a present for him. A long gold chain with a St Christopher medal attached. She even had the medal engraved with his name: DEREK MOODY. How annoyed she'd been when he seemed embarrassed to wear it. 'Oh, come on, Maxine! A holy medal!'

Yet he'd never once taken it off after that day.

He was laughing as the photo was taken, his face full of mischief. He'd once always been like that. Then he'd grown up, gone to high school, met the wrong people and everything had changed. But his face in the photograph didn't look as if it was hiding any troubles. Mum's eyes lingered on it, remembering too. Her mouth turned up at the corners, a faint hint of a smile.

She never smiles like that at me, Maxine thought.

Then she kissed her fingertips and placed them lovingly against the glass.

There was a lump in Maxine's throat as she watched. Mum repeated the same thing every single day, more love in that simple gesture than she had displayed to Maxine for so long. She didn't even bother looking back at her as she went out the door.

What was the use of trying when they didn't really care what she did? Or where she went? When they wished, her mother especially, that it hadn't been Derek who had disappeared. When they wished it had been Maxine.

Well, she wasn't going to try any longer.

It had been a long time since she'd challenged the Mighty Zola.

Today they would do battle again!

CHAPTER FOUR

Why did she always feel she was being watched? Guilt, she told herself, as she hurried through the back streets towards Simmy's. She stopped once and looked around. There were people on the street, a line waiting at a distant bus stop ... a man in his garden arguing with a garden gnome. No one seemed even vaguely interested in her. And yet ... She shivered and scrutinised everyone again. Someone *was* watching her. That feeling was so strong.

'Not seen you for a while.' Simmy's son, Taft, was as fat as his father, his great wobbly bulk covered by a stain-encrusted overall. 'Been grounded?'

Maxine didn't answer. Instead she pointed out one particular stain on his front. 'Enjoy your tomato soup last night?' She grinned. 'Or was it something Bolognese?'

He looked puzzled as she ran to the Mighty Zola. It would take him all day to figure that one out.

Mighty Zola was not alone. He was already fighting a deadly battle with a lethal opponent. And losing! Maxine's name as Champion had been replaced.

She stiffened when she saw exactly who had replaced her and was even now topping the total of points against his name.

Cam.

'What are you doing here?' She snapped the question out angrily, as if he had no right to be here at all. Which, she decided, he hadn't! 'Aren't you supposed to be at school?'

He didn't interrupt his battle with Zola. His eyes only glanced in her direction for a second. 'I could ask you the same question.'

'I got time off, if you must know.'

He lifted an eyebrow, though he never lost concentration on his game. 'What for? Good behaviour?'

'What are you doing here anyway? I've never seen you at Simmy's before.' It wasn't Cam's kind of place.

'I have time off too,' he said, scoring another twenty points. 'For study.'

'Well, then, shouldn't you be studying?'

'I don't need to study. I'm really clever. Didn't you know?'

This was obviously Cam trying to be funny.

'You think you're something. Really clever! Ha!'

But he was. Really brilliant at this game too. She watched fascinated as points piled upon points. She'd never seen anyone react so quickly, and she realised with a sinking heart that she was jealous. Jealous of Cam? How depressing!

'I'm going to be a pilot one day,' he said, as if to explain his expertise in the game.

'Oh, that will be wonderful,' Maxine said, very deliberately. 'You'll be able to deliver the carryouts so much quicker. Not so much takeaways ... as flyaways.' She began to giggle.

Her silly remark shot home. He missed an important shot and the Mighty Zola emerged triumphant on the screen. Maxine felt suddenly sick. What a horrible, nasty thing to say! She wanted to apologise, but couldn't find the words.

Cam turned on her. 'Goodness, that sounds like something your brother would have said. He hasn't disappeared at all. You've just taken over from him.'

All her regret disappeared in a flash. Apologise to

him? He could be as cruel as she any day. She hated him! She hated everybody! He strode from the machine and she called after him, 'Away with you back to Hong Kong where you belong!'

That remark didn't bother him a bit. He turned back to her for a second, shaking his head. 'Don't be stupid, Maxine. I was born two streets away from you.'

And with that he was off, whistling. He had won. Not only against the Mighty Zola, but also against her.

The day did not improve. She couldn't beat Cam's score, no matter how she tried. She couldn't concentrate, and her resentment just kept building up. She ate a hot dog for lunch, standing with all the other truants behind the disused Portakabins in town. Then she spent the afternoon on one of the creaky old swings in a playground.

It was here that Father Matthew found her. 'Maxine Moody? I thought that was you.'

She almost fell off the swing at the sound of his voice. 'On your way home from school?'

She realised with relief that it was just about time for school to come out. She nodded silently.

He looked around the deserted playground. 'Do you come here to think?' He didn't wait for an answer. 'You come to church sometimes for the same thing. I disturbed you that last time. I'm sorry. I didn't mean to.' He waited. He wanted Maxine to talk to him. To confide in him.

'I'll have to go.' Maxine was already on her feet, moving away from him. 'Mum and Dad worry when I'm late.' Always the same feeble excuse.

He called after her, 'Maxine, if you ever want to talk, that's what I'm here for. Remember that, won't you?'

Yes, sure, she thought as she raced from the playground. Everyone wanted her to talk to them. Trouble was, no one ever wanted to listen.

She almost didn't go home. When she turned the corner into her street, there was a police car outside her house.

They knew!

Miss Ross or one of the other teachers (they were all the same!) had told on her again. This time, her parents had had enough of her. They were putting her away. Her father had once told her, in a temper, that 'next time' he would have her taken into care. She was 'beyond parental control'. There had been many 'next times' since then. Maybe today had been the last straw. She drew herself up to her full height and set her

33

shoulders straight. Face the music, kiddo, she told herself. Maybe in a home someone will care what happens to you.

In fact, her parents weren't interested in whether she'd been to school or not. They had something – someone – more important on their minds.

Derek.

As she came in the door, her father approached her.

'You're going to stay with Mrs Templeton for a few days, Maxine.' Mrs Templeton. Handy neighbour to have when you wanted to be rid of an unwanted daughter.

She looked past her father to where her mother sat in the armchair in the living room. She was crying, being comforted by a policewoman kneeling in front of her.

'Why?' Maxine asked. 'Where are you going? What's wrong?'

Why can't all three of us go together? she wanted to ask. Share whatever it is.

'Your mother and I are going to London.' Suddenly he gripped her by the shoulders and bent down so his eyes, dark and flecked with green like her own, were level with hers. There were tears in them. Held back, but there, trying not to brim over. 'We have to be very strong, Maxine. So I'm going to tell you. The police have found a body.'

His voice broke at that point, and he had to repeat it. '... a body. They think it might be Derek. They think it probably is. I have to go ... and identify ...' His voice broke again. The tears almost did brim over and he had to swallow them back. 'I just want you to prepare yourself, but we think Derek is dead.'

CHAPTER FIVE

Had it really been two months since that awful day? Two months when all she'd felt was guilt and pain and remorse. She had wished her brother dead, and then suddenly he was. She spent a lot of her time during those months in church, lighting enough candles to illuminate Blackpool. Father Matthew would approach her. She knew he wanted to offer words of comfort to her, let her pour out her heart to him. Now, more than ever, she needed someone to talk to. But not him.

Not a priest.

She couldn't lie to a priest. And there was a feeling in her worse than all the guilt and all the remorse. One she could never confess to anyone.

Relief.

She tried not to feel it. Tried to push it down, deep into her soul, whenever it surfaced. But it wouldn't stay down for long, like a cork bobbing to the surface of a river.

Relief.

Derek was dead. Maybe now they would have time for her. Maybe now Derek would be put in the past – where he belonged! They would realise Maxine was here. Alive. With them.

She tried so hard to be good in those weeks after the funeral. A dutiful daughter, comforting her grieving mother.

And how she grieved. If she had cried when Derek had disappeared, she sobbed bitterly now. The funeral itself had been a nightmare, an ordeal Maxine just wanted to forget. Her mother almost collapsing; her father having to help her, sobbing, from the church.

'Is Mum going to be all right, Dad?' she had asked him many times.

He had cried too. Silently. Tears would run down his face as he stood making dinner for them, or as he sat pretending to read the evening paper.

'Of course she will,' he had assured her, pulling her close to him. It had been so long since he'd held her like that, and the relief burst onto the surface again.

Derek was dead. And she was glad!

'We have to let her cry,' he would say. 'It's best to grieve, Maxine. The funeral was the time for her to let Derek rest. To close the door. He'll never be away from us, of course, but now he's in another room. Your mother will accept that eventually, and then, soon, we'll all begin to live again.'

They would begin to live again. She had never felt so happy as she did that night, or so guilty.

She was wicked. There was no other word for someone who could feel like this. But when she felt her dad's arms around her, heard him say they would 'begin to live again', she didn't care.

She even wrote it down and kept the note under her pillow.

But when would they begin to live again?

As the weeks dragged by, nothing changed. If anything, things got worse.

'You've got to give your mother time,' Miss Ross told her. 'It's a hard thing to accept. Death.'

'But Dad said ...' She didn't have to continue. She had told Miss Ross so often, she knew what she was going to say.

'Think how hard it must be for him. You all prayed for Derek to come back.'

Maxine turned away, sure it must show on her face that she hadn't.

'And suddenly,' Miss Ross went on, 'to discover that he'd been dead for months.'

That had hurt them. Maxine knew that. All the weeks and months they had hoped for him to walk in the door, he had been dead. Lying for all those months in a burnt-out building that squatters and the homeless used.

'Give them time, Maxine.'

But it seemed all the time in the world wouldn't be enough for her mother.

Maxine came home from school one day to find the house a hive of activity. Mum was polishing the front room, Dad was arranging chairs around a table. His face was drawn, and he looked up at Maxine with sad eyes.

'Are we having visitors?' she asked.

For a moment her hopes rose. Visitors were something they never had now. Visitors would mean a return to normal living. Back to what they once were. 'Are we, Mum? Are we having visitors?'

Her mum's face glowed. Her eyes were bright. Maxine hadn't seen her like that for so long. Yet it didn't look right somehow.

'No one who would interest you, Maxine. In fact, perhaps you could go out with your friends tonight.'

Now she wanted rid of her? Why?

'Who's coming?' she insisted.

It was her father who answered her. 'We're having a fortune teller, Maxine.'

Mum slammed the polish down on the table. 'I told you before. She's not a fortune teller. She's a medium.' She turned to Maxine. 'I'm having a seance, dear.' Her tone defied Maxine to disapprove.

'But ... why ...?'

'Exactly!' her father snapped. 'Why? It's a crazy idea. Why can't you put it all in the past, Gill?'

'I can't do it as easily as you can, obviously.'

'There is no point to this! Derek is dead!'

Her mother put her hands over her ears. 'Shut up! I won't hear you say that.'

Maxine began to back out. They had forgotten she was there. Derek was dead, but his memory still filled their lives, leaving no room for her.

She lay on the bed listening to their voices downstairs, still arguing. Nothing was going to change. Nothing was ever going to change.

She must have dozed off, drifting into an uneasy

sleep, dreaming she was playing and running and chasing someone. Her laughter, her giggles suddenly turned to anger. She pushed hard and whoever she was chasing, fell. And as they fell, their arms flailing wildly, the face all at once became clear. Derek! She could never see him when awake or remember his features. Yet here, in her nightmare, she saw him clearly. His eyes accused her as he tumbled down, reaching out for her hand. And try as she might, she couldn't move. Couldn't lift a finger to help him.

She awoke with a start, little beads of sweat on her brow, her face flushed. Thank heaven she was awake!

The phone was ringing. 'I'll get it,' she called downstairs.

The house was quiet now. The early-evening sun darting in and out of clouds sent shafts of light along the landing.

She picked up the extension outside her bedroom. 'Hello?'

She waited for an answer. Someone was there. She could hear them breathing. Short, nervous breaths. 'Hello?' she said again.

'Maxie ...?'

No one had ever called her that except ...

'Yes, it's Maxine. Who's this?'

There was another pause and at precisely that second the sun appeared from behind a cloud and light exploded along the hallway. Maxine was always to remember that moment.

'Maxie. It's me ... it's Derek.'

CHAPTER SIX

Maxine slammed down the phone. She began to shake and couldn't stop.

Was she still dreaming? That was her first thought. That she was still lying on her bed, having a nightmare. Any moment now, she would wake up. She had to. She stared at her trembling hands.

No. It wasn't a dream, or a nightmare. She *was* standing here on the upstairs landing, and Derek had just phoned her.

NO! NO! NO!

That couldn't be. Derek was dead.

'It's me, Derek.' Had that been Derek's voice? She couldn't remember how his voice had sounded, but she was sure it had never been so deep.

And, of course, it *couldn't* be Derek. What was she thinking about?

Yet ... Derek had always called her Maxie; he was the only one who ever had.

Someone was playing tricks on her. Who could be so cruel? Could anyone?

Maybe there had been no phone call. It had all been in her imagination. Yet here she was standing at the phone, hands still trembling on the receiver.

'It's me, Derek ...'

There must be hundreds of boys called Derek. It wasn't an unusual name. This was just another of them. A wrong number. Another Derek.

'Maxie.' He had called her Maxie! What were the chances of another Derek having a sister called Maxie?

What was going on? Who had it been?

Suddenly the phone began ringing again. Maxine almost screamed. He was phoning back!

'I'll get it, Maxine.'

Her mother was padding across the hallway to the phone downstairs.

No! She mustn't answer it. That would be too cruel. Mum had been through enough.

Maxine grabbed for the receiver and lifted it, shouting at the same time, 'Got it, Mum. I've got it.'

The footsteps stopped. 'Fine, dear. Who is it?'

Maxine held the receiver far away from her ear. She didn't want to hear that voice again. Didn't want to speak.

'Hello? Hello? Is anybody there?'

It was her gran. Maxine almost screeched with delight. 'Gran! It's great hearing from you.'

'Goodness, you sound pleased to hear my voice. If I'd thought I'd get a welcome like this, I would have phoned sooner.'

Her gran was wonderful. She had some strange job where she used flip charts and gave 'motivational' talks to business people. She was always jetting off to one foreign place or another. If she lived closer, or stayed in one place for any length of time, Maxine was sure she would be able to talk to her, to tell her things. Her gran was smart.

'I'm actually phoning from Sydney. I just wondered how your mum is.'

'Who is it, Maxine?' Mum called.

'You can ask her yourself, Gran.' She shouted downstairs, 'It's Gran.' She giggled. 'She's phoning from Sydney's.'

Before her mum picked up the receiver, Gran said softly, 'Are you managing all right, dear?'

If Mum hadn't been on the line, Maxine might have told her about the phone call. Gran's common sense would have made everything normal. But Mum was there now. It was impossible to speak. 'I'm fine, Gran. Honest. Love you.'

'Love you too, sweetheart.'

She put down the phone. Her hands had stopped shaking. Gran's sensible voice coming down the line had made that other voice seem an age away. Unreal somehow. She didn't want to think about it.

'Bet you didn't tell your mother about this fortune teller coming!' Dad said sharply when Mum finally came off the phone. Mum's face flushed and Maxine knew he was right.

'No. Of course you didn't. Because you know exactly what your mother would have said. Voodoo mumbo jumbo nonsense!'

'You don't agree with it, Jim,' Mum said softly. 'But you promised you wouldn't interfere. You promised.'

His face lost its anger. Tenderness filled it again. He touched his wife's hand.

'You know I won't. I don't want you to do it.' He sighed. 'But I'll stay with you.'

Mum lifted his hand and held it against her cheek. And Maxine, standing watching them from the doorway, couldn't remember the last time she'd seen her mother making such a loving gesture to her dad.

The fortune teller – medium – didn't look a bit like Maxine had expected. She was bursting out of the flowery dress she was wearing, which was also far too short for her. She had obviously just finished her late-night shopping at the freezer centre and she pushed the bags at Maxine. 'Put these in the freezer for me, hen. I don't want my thighs defrosted.'

Her dad had started to cough at that – trying to stifle a giggle. Maxine almost giggled too.

'By the way,' the medium said, 'my name is Luella Oribine.'

Luella Oribine. Maxine ran the name around her tongue. It had a ring to it.

'Are we in here, hen?' She followed Mum into the dining room, waving Maxine and her frozen thighs away to the kitchen.

When Maxine returned, the medium was lighting a cigarette without even asking if she could smoke. And Mum didn't even give her any trouble. Maxine saw Dad glare at her. He was always sent out into the garden with his pipe whenever he wanted to smoke.

He motioned Maxine back into the kitchen. 'Do you believe her?' he whispered when the door was safely closed. 'I know what I'd like to do with her frozen thighs.' They were both giggling as Luella Oribine popped her head round the kitchen door.

'Are you coming, Mr Moody? I feel the vibes very strong tonight. Who knows, I might have a message for you as well.' It was an order, not a suggestion.

Dad looked at Maxine. 'I suppose I have to.' He turned again to Maxine at the door. 'I think we should fasten our safety belts, honey ... we're in for a bumpy night.'

CHAPTER SEVEN

Maxine stayed upstairs while the seance went ahead. She expected to hear weird noises, moans, ghostly voices. Instead, all she heard, quite clearly, was the strident tones of Luella Oribine.

'I have a message for you, Mr Moody. From your father. He's a happy man. He always knew there was a heaven and now he's in it.'

Bunkum! thought Maxine. She could just picture her dad's expression as he listened. Incredulous, biting his lip to keep from laughing out loud.

There were messages from aunts and uncles. Even neighbours who had 'passed into the spirit world', as she put it. According to Luella they were all crowding round her trying to get messages through. Every so often she would break off communications and scold one of them for their impatience.

'I'm telling you for the last time! Shove me once more and you're at the back of the queue!'

Maxine ended up sitting in the kitchen so she could hear better. This was more fun than she had expected. I bet Dad is desperate to giggle, she thought. But he wouldn't. This was too important to Mum, and there was only one message she wanted to hear.

Finally, it came.

'Ah, your boy ... that's who you're waiting for, isn't it?'

Maxine held her breath. Surely she wasn't really going to bring a message from Derek?

Mum's voice trembled as she answered. 'He was alone. He ... died alone ... I want him to know ... we cared ... how much we cared ...' Her voice broke. She was crying. Maxine couldn't quite hear her father's murmured words of comfort.

'He understands.' Luella's voice was gentle now. She sounded so different.

'He wants me to tell you. He loves you. He always did.' Then her voice became so low and indistinct that Maxine could no longer make out what she was saying.

Finally she heard her say, 'He wants you to be happy. To get on with your life. For his sake. That's the important thing now.'

Yes! Yes! Maybe this fortune teller hadn't been such a crazy idea after all. If she made Mum forget about the past and get on with her life.

'He says he loves you all. And he's very happy where he is.'

Her mother's voice when she answered that was almost a whisper. But there was so much relief in her words. 'Is he? Is he honestly?'

Luella Oribine left soon afterwards. The gentle voice was gone. She was back to what Maxine felt was her usual self, cigarette in her mouth, demanding her frozen thighs. Maxine had by this time decided she liked her and smiled broadly as she handed them over.

Dad's attitude too seemed to have changed. He shook her hand warmly.

'Thank you. I appreciate what you said tonight.'

She took the cigarette out of her mouth and smiled. 'I hope it helps. She has to get on with her life. There's so much sadness here.' She looked around and her eyes rested on Maxine. A puzzled frown settled on her face. One that Maxine couldn't understand.

Then she shook her head and turned back to Dad. 'If you ever need me again, you know where to find me.'

Dad closed the door thoughtfully.

'Dad, was that really Derek giving her a message?'

He looked up at Maxine's question. He sighed, and took a while to answer. Finally he straightened up. 'Bunkum!' he snapped. 'But if it helps your mum, Maxine, if it gets things back to normal around here, I don't care. I just don't care!'

Over the next few days, Maxine forgot about the phone call. Began to imagine it had never really happened. Mum seemed better too. Elated almost. For the first few days after the seance Maxine was happier than she'd been in a long time. But it wasn't to last.

Saturday was a beautiful day. Dad was out playing golf, Mum was in the kitchen fitting new shelves. Maxine had a lie-in and was still half asleep as she came downstairs. She heard her mother murmuring something and expected to see someone with her when she entered the kitchen. But the room was empty.

'Is this even?' Mum held the shelf for Maxine to judge.

'Looks even to me. Who was here? I heard you talking to someone.'

Mum didn't even look at her. 'Derek,' she said, as if it was the most natural thing in the world. 'Derek is here.'

Maxine felt the blood drain from her face. What was happening to her mum?

Her mum turned to her, her face radiant. 'I'm not going crazy. I know he's ... well, I know he isn't here in the physical sense.' She smiled. 'But since the seance, I've felt him so close, watching me. With me. My son.'

Maxine wanted to cry. Instead she shouted, 'There's no one here, Mum. I'm here! I'm the only one who's here!'

Her mother was hardly listening. 'Have you ever felt sometimes that someone was watching you? I've felt that for a long time now.'

Maxine shivered. How often had she felt that? Was this the explanation? The ghost of her dead brother had been watching over them all along? Her mother had no doubt anyway.

'Now I know the reason. Derek. The seance brought him back to me, and now ... I'm never going to lose him again.'

Maxine ran from the house in tears. She was never going to be rid of Derek. Even in death, he was pushing her out of her mother's life!

I hate him! I hate him! She almost screamed it aloud,

running, where to she didn't know. People looked at her in annoyance as she plummeted into them and then ran on without a word.

Suddenly there were footsteps behind her, closing in on her. Hands grabbed at her shoulders, whirling her around. 'Maxine, what's wrong?'

It was Cam, looking genuinely worried about her. Cam! He was clever. Cam would understand what was going on. He would know what to do. Cam would help her. She was going to tell Cam everything!

CHAPTER EIGHT

They went to a nearby café and there, Maxine poured it all out to him.

'My mother says the very worst thing that can happen is to lose a child,' Cam told her when she'd finished. 'Your mum's lost Derek twice. Just think what she must be going through.'

Maxine almost stormed out of the café then. 'Whose side are you on? I only told you because I thought you'd know how to help me.'

'You have to understand your mother's feelings. Be patient.'

'I'm fed up being patient. Understanding. I want someone to understand me for a change.'

'I understand.' Cam pulled her back into her seat. 'I wouldn't like it either.'

Maxine slumped down. 'She gave me the creeps,

Cam. She's making me feel he's there in the house. A ghost. And what about that phone call? Do you think it *was* Derek? It was strange I got the phone call the same night we had a seance. Maybe he came back to give Luella Oribine that message.'

He looked at her as if she was crazy. 'Don't be stupid. Ghosts don't make phone calls.'

'Well ... who then?'

'A crank. Someone who doesn't like you ...' He shrugged. 'And there's plenty of those about.'

Was this him trying to be funny again? It was hard to tell when he didn't even smile.

'Someone who's just plain nasty.'

For a second a picture of Sweeney came into her head. Sweeney who was always watching her with a sneer. Sweeney, who might not pick on a girl openly, but could think up just such a devious plan to frighten her.

Cam was still talking. 'When things like this happen, cranks come out of the woodwork. I'm surprised you haven't had more.'

Maxine interrupted him excitedly. 'Maybe we have, Cam.'

She was remembering calls now. Long silent calls,

when she would shout down the line, 'Who's there?' And never receive an answer. She knew someone was there. She could remember the breathing, quick, nervous breathing, just like the other day. Then whoever it was would hang up and the line would go dead.

'Just since Derek has died?' Cam asked.

Maxine nodded. 'Yes. Over the past few weeks. Do you think I should tell my parents?'

'Wait until you get another one,' Cam said. '*If* you get another one. But just tell your dad. Not your mum.' He hesitated, but she could imagine what he'd been about to say. Her mum was potty enough already.

She wasn't. Maxine almost told him. But she was near the edge of some kind of madness, even Maxine could see that.

'And if you get another,' Cam said slowly, as if he was explaining something to a stupid child, 'dial 1471 to find out where they're calling from. I don't know why you didn't do that the last time.'

Typical Cam! 'When you get a phone call from your dead brother you're not exactly thinking straight, smart alec!'

He smirked. The nearest thing she'd ever seen to a smile on his face. 'OK, OK, keep your hair on.'

She planned to tell Dad anyway about her mother talking to Derek. That was scary. But when she came home she didn't have to tell him anything. He already knew. That was clear from the vacant look on his face when she went into the living room.

'I knew that seance was a mistake,' he said at once. 'Heard the latest? She can feel Derek touching her hair as she passes him. He's with her all the time now.' For a moment, Maxine felt they were together, that he too knew the feeling she had been experiencing for so long ... being shut out because of the memory of Derek. For the first time since her brother had gone, she didn't feel so alone. Maybe now she had her father.

'So ... what are we going to do about it, Dad?'

He looked at her, puzzled. 'Do? We're not going to do anything. She's happy. For the first time she seems happy. If it's not going to do her any harm, if it helps her ... what's the point of doing anything?'

All Maxine's hopes evaporated with those words. She was alone again.

'If it helps her cope,' her dad went on. 'I don't care ...'

After that, Mum took to visiting other fortune tellers – mediums. (She would correct Maxine every time.) She

58

returned happier with every visit. Maxine simply didn't know what to do. If life had been hard before, it was impossible now.

Hard at home, and hard at school. All the talk there was about Paul Wilson. He had finally given up coming to school and his parents had moved him somewhere else. Sweeney was jubilant. He had won again. He swaggered about the playground looking for his next victim, and every pupil avoided him. They didn't want to be next.

'How does he get away with it?' Maxine said to Cam as they watched him. 'He never seems to be the one to suffer.'

'He's devious,' Cam said. 'Careful who he picks on. Haven't you noticed? Always the boys who come from good family backgrounds. With caring parents and settled family lives.'

Maxine wasn't sure she understood what he meant. 'Why should that make a difference?'

'When your parents went to the headmaster to complain about Sweeney, can you remember what they were told?'

And she could. She had overheard her angry parents discuss it in the living room the day they came back from seeing him. 'Yes,' she said. 'Sweeney comes from a deprived background. A broken home. We have to make allowances for him.'

Cam agreed. 'So he gets away with it every time. A suspension, a black mark on his record, and then he's back worse than ever.'

Yes, Sweeney had made Derek's life even more of a hell when he'd returned after the suspension he got for tormenting Derek.

Now, with Paul Wilson gone, Sweeney needed a new victim. Someone else to torment. Well, it certainly wasn't going to be her!

'Is everything all right, Maxine?' Miss Ross asked her one day in English. She was supposed to be reading *King Lear*. How could anybody enjoy such tripe?

Maxine jumped at the sound of her voice. 'I'm fine.'

Miss Ross obviously wasn't convinced. 'Come and see me after class,' she said.

After the lesson Maxine stood alone in front of her teacher's desk. Miss Ross stacked exercise books neatly together before she even looked up.

'What is wrong with you, Maxine? You've been so distracted lately. Is everything OK at home?'

Miss Ross had been kind. She had hardly left Maxine's side all through the bad times of the funeral. She would understand, even if it would sound weird.

'It's Derek ...'

'But we discussed this, Maxine. It will take your mother time to come to terms with his death.'

'I don't think he is dead,' Maxine muttered.

Miss Ross's collection of exercise books collapsed all over her desk. 'What on earth do you mean?'

'He isn't dead. He wanders around our house every day with my mum.'

Miss Ross went deathly pale. She must be beginning to think my family's one sandwich short of a picnic, Maxine thought.

She went on quickly to explain. She knew she better had before Miss Ross fainted. 'My mum had a seance. Now she's sure she's brought Derek back from the other side. That he's with her all the time. It's awful, Miss Ross.'

'That isn't healthy, Maxine.'

'I know. But Dad says this is helping Mum cope.'

'But you don't think it is, do you?'

How wise of Miss Ross to see exactly how she felt! Her anger at everything erupted. 'No! I think it's stupid

61

and crazy. Derek's dead. And that should be the end of it!'

She was still angry when she went home. Still angry when the phone rang just before tea.

'Hello?'

For a moment there was no answer, only that ominous breathing. Maxine felt her heart beat faster, began to sweat. 'Hello!' She snapped the word out.

Then the voice, very low, very soft. 'Maxie ... it's me, Derek ...'

Her anger didn't let him say another word. She began yelling down the line.

'No, you're not! You're a crank, a vicious, wicked crank. You're not my brother! My brother's dead. And ... I'M GLAD HE IS!'

There was a long pause. The line went dead. Whoever it was had slammed the receiver down, shocked by her words.

Good, she thought. That will be the end of that. Now he won't phone again.

She stood for a moment breathing hard. What had Cam told her? Dial 1471. Find out where that phone call came from.

She did. It was a pay phone somewhere in the town. 'Press 3 if you wish to redial this number,' a clinical voice informed her.

Maxine pressed 3.

She hoped this mysterious caller would still be there. She would have something to say to him, whoever he was. Had it been Sweeney? It hadn't sounded like him, but he could make his cronies do anything. Perhaps it had been one of them.

The phone rang for a long time. So long that she was just about to hang up when suddenly the receiver was picked up.

'Hello? Who's this?'

The voice was a woman's.

'I wonder if you could help me. I've just had a call from this number ...'

The woman cackled. 'That would be a miracle, dearie.'

'It was from a boy,' Maxine explained slowly. 'Is there a boy anywhere around there?'

'Probably plenty of them, dearie.' The woman was drunk. Maxine was convinced of that now.

'Does anyone live near this phone box?' She tried not to sound irritated.

'Not a single soul,' the woman replied. 'But people are dying to move here.'

Maxine waited as patiently as she could for the woman to stop laughing. She began to think this was the pay phone at the local mental hospital.

'Can you give me the address of this pay phone, please?' Now she didn't care if she sounded rude or not.

Finally, the woman stopped laughing. Her voice came through loud and clear. And Maxine wished she hadn't heard her.

'This is the cemetery, dearie. You've got through to the phone box at the cemetery.'

CHAPTER NINE

There are no such things as ghosts.

Ghosts don't make phone calls.

She stood by the phone telling herself that over and over again. It didn't stop her shaking. The phone call had come from the cemetery. She knew the phone box the woman was talking about. Near the crematorium, not far from the war memorial, meant for mourners who wanted to call a taxi or phone for a lift. It was never meant for residents! It was amazing that it was actually working, as it was usually vandalised by the groups of youths who roamed the cemetery, desecrating gravestones, drinking, hiding from truancy officers. And of course, that was the explanation. Some nasty boy meaning to hurt, to scare, to make her wonder if ...

No! Ghosts don't make phone calls. They have other means of communication. Like Luella Oribine.

Yet, another part of her mind said, what if Luella had brought him back? Brought Derek back from the other side ... what if it really was Derek who ... ?

No! It was a crank. It had to be. Just as Cam had said. What a cruel trick to play on anyone! And again she thought of Sweeney. Just the kind of scary, wicked tactic he would think up. But why?

She dialled Cam's number. It was his grandmother who answered and Maxine groaned. She was as eccentric as Maxine's mother, and her accent was so thick it took them ten minutes to figure out what the other was saying. Finally Maxine deduced that Cam was working for his father tonight, delivering takeaways. Just her luck!

Unless she ordered a meal, there was no way she was going to catch him tonight.

So, maybe it was Fate that sent Father Matthew to the house that evening. He arrived after tea, just as Mum was stacking the dishwasher and Dad was asking Maxine once again why she was so quiet. He had noticed her pallor as soon as he'd come home. Assumed she was in for some bug or other.

Father Matthew looked uneasy as he entered the

living room. Maxine could understand why. Since the seance, Mum had hardly been to church. Her life had been overtaken by spiritualist meetings and yet more seances.

She who had been a constant visitor to the church, lighting candles, never missing mass, had found something else. Something that brought her closer to her beloved son.

Maxine's father realised at once why the priest had come. 'She'll come back to the church, Father. Just give her time. Once she comes to terms with Derek's ...' He couldn't bring himself to say the word 'death'. 'She'll be OK. This is helping her. That's why I'm not saying too much about it.'

Father Matthew's voice was soft. 'But is it? This is unhealthy, this obsession. It can't be helping her.'

Mum came in from the kitchen and heard him. 'Unhealthy? This is the best thing that has happened to me since Derek disappeared. I feel ... he's with me all the time. And I like it!'

'His memory should be with you, Mrs Moody. But not his presence. He's in another place now, and we should leave him there.'

'I don't want him anywhere else but here, with me!

That's where he belongs!' Mum shouted at Father Matthew. Maxine was shocked. 'You couldn't bring him to me. That's why you're so annoyed.'

She turned her back on the priest then, dismissing him. Father Matthew's voice was gentle as ever. 'I'll always be here if you need me, Mrs Moody.' His eyes moved around the room and came to rest on Maxine. 'If any of you need me.'

'Maxine,' her father said, already moving to his wife's side. 'Will you see Father Matthew out?'

He was being asked to leave, but he didn't seem to mind. He smiled and followed Maxine to the door.

'I'm sorry, Father,' she said.

'No need to apologise. You should hear the way some people talk to me.' He smiled and Maxine smiled back. 'But I did mean what I said. I am here if you ever want to talk.'

Talk? She almost told him then and there about the phone calls, but he would think she was as crazy as her mother. Instead, she asked him, 'Father, do you believe in ghosts?'

'Ghosts?' He shook his head. 'Although I think you can feel the presence of a loved one, and that can comfort you.'

'But isn't that what Mum's doing?'

Again he shook his head. 'No. Not like your mum. Derek's presence isn't comforting her. It's taking over her life. She isn't letting him rest in peace.'

And Derek wasn't giving her any peace either. Even dead, he was more important to her parents than Maxine. Loved more than her, cared about more than she was.

'Are you allowed to hate a dead person?' she asked, knowing what his answer would be.

'You don't hate him, Maxine. Hate is a useless emotion. Negative. Doesn't get you anywhere. Pray for him, and get on with your life. You're young, you should be enjoying yourself.' He touched her shoulder. 'Don't give up on your mum. And don't you worry about ghosts either. There are no such things as ghosts.'

There are no such things as ghosts. So the phone calls were just cruel tricks. And what if her mother were to answer one of those calls? She might really believe it *was* Derek. Oh no! Maxine couldn't risk that. She had to tell Dad. It was the only thing to do, she decided. He would know what to do about those calls. And it was comforting to know they would be doing something together, to protect Mum.

She waited until that night when he came in to say goodnight to her. Mum was already in bed.

'Dad, can I talk to you?'

He smiled and sat down on the bed beside her.

'Do you believe in ghosts?' She had to ask. She wanted his common sense to reassure her.

'Oh, don't you start, Maxine! One in the family's enough.'

She was saying it all wrong. She knew it. But what other way was there to explain? 'But, Dad ... I've been getting these phone calls.'

'Phone calls? What kind of phone calls?'

She hesitated for a long time before she answered him. 'From Derek,' she said finally. She wanted him to tell her it was nonsense. She wanted him to tell her it was the vicious trick of a crank.

He pushed his hands through his hair. 'What! What's this?'

She went on quickly, trying to explain. 'From someone who says he's Derek.'

He didn't let her go on. He stood up. He didn't shout at her, but his low voice was even worse than a yell. 'Is this another of your pathetic attempts to get attention? Isn't it enough I've got your mother to pull through this, without you starting your nonsense too?'

She tried to protest. He wouldn't listen. Why wouldn't they ever listen?

'If I hear you mention one word of this nonsense to your mother!' He looked as if he was ready to cry. Maybe her mother wasn't the only one who was on the edge. 'You'd think you would be a help to me, Maxine. Instead, you're nothing but a hindrance.'

She wanted to cry. It was so unfair. She had only wanted to protect her mum, and now, as usual, she was getting the blame for everything. Crying never did any good. So instead she shouted at him. 'Derek would be a marvellous help, of course! Wonderful Derek! Maybe you'd rather it was me who was dead, instead of him? Well, now at least you've got your beloved Derek back!'

Her father put his hands over his ears to blot out her words. 'Shut up!' he shouted. 'Your mother'll hear you.'

And then he was gone, out of the room, closing the door softly behind him. More anger in that silence than in any scream.

She'd never try to talk to him again, she promised herself. She'd never tell him anything. What was the use? They never listened. She was alone. She'd never felt quite so alone before.

Father Matthew was right. She was going to live her life, and when that crank called again she was going to call his bluff. She was going to pretend she believed him. She was going to meet this boy who said he was Derek.

CHAPTER TEN

She didn't go to school next day. Instead, she and the Mighty Zola battled it out. Her concentration was gone, however, for she hardly won a game. Cam's name still appeared triumphantly above her own. Mighty Champion. She began to shake the machine, urging the game to go in her favour.

'Hey! Hey, you!' Suddenly Simmy's son, Taft, was wobbling towards her. 'What do you think you're playing at?'

'I'm playing the Mighty Zola!' she snapped. 'What does it look like?'

He stood his ground, hands on hips, glaring at her. She glanced at the cartoon picture of Zola on the screen, standing in exactly that way, bronze muscles rippling. Then she looked back at Taft. Eggs must have been on the menu for lunch, and some kind of baked beans. Shreds of them were encrusted, probably for ever, down the front of his T-shirt. Mighty Zola and Taft, his flabby imitation. Maxine began to giggle.

'What's so funny?' Taft demanded.

Maxine pointed at the machine. 'Mighty Zola' – then she turned her finger on Taft – 'and tubby Taft!' She laughed again.

Taft took an angry step towards her. 'I'm going to phone the school on you,' he threatened. 'Aren't you supposed to be there?'

'Phone them,' Maxine said, standing her ground. 'Of course, they'll let the police know I'm underage and shouldn't be in here at all, and they'll shut this place down.'

His brow furrowed, trying to figure it out. 'You just get out of here. Right now!' he finally decided. 'And don't come back. 'Cause we won't let you in.'

She swung her rucksack over her shoulder and almost knocked him off his feet.

'Yes, you will,' she said, sure of herself. 'As long as I have money to spend on the Mighty Zola you'll let me in!'

She felt his eyes bore into her back as she strode from the arcade. She wasn't afraid of Taft ... he was nothing.

Though why was she always so cruel to him? She had never used to be this cruel.

'It's a pity it was only your brother that disappeared. Too bad you didn't disappear along with him.'

She froze and turned to face him. There was real malice in Taft's voice and in his look. His voice sounded different too. Someone had been making those phone calls. Someone who didn't like her. Who was trying to frighten her. Could that someone be Taft? She wasn't afraid of him. But maybe she should be.

When she left the arcade she walked, without thinking where she was going. As far away from school as possible. She had so much on her mind. Eventually she stopped and found herself standing across the street from the cemetery. Wasn't that strange? she thought. She hadn't meant to come here ... had she?

There are no such things as accidents, she had once read. Everything was kismet, everything that happened was meant to be.

Maxine didn't hesitate. She crossed the street and entered through the big green gates that opened onto the long path.

The cemetery was huge. A dark, shady place even

in daylight. Drunks slept in the old Victorian mausoleums that stood almost hidden by trees. Gangs roamed up here in the darkness, vandalising the gravestones. It was a great hiding place for children too with its monkey-puzzle trees shutting out the sunlight, and bushes of rhododendrons covering every path. She remembered that she and Derek had often walked up here. Exploring. Derek loved reading the old gravestones, and he used to enjoy sketching the ornately carved mausoleums. Those were the good times, when she and her brother had got on well. Before everything changed.

'The dead can't harm us, Maxine,' he used to tell her, whenever the sun went behind a cloud and the sky darkened ominously.

She had never been afraid here. Until now.

Yet she couldn't stop walking deeper inside.

She passed the phone box, situated on the crossroads between the war memorial and the crematorium. The phone box was constantly vandalised and graffiti was scratched and daubed over the walls.

'SOMEBODY MIGHT HAVE HAD THE DECENCY TO BURY ME WITH A MOBILE PHONE,' some wag had written.

Maxine carried on, wondering why anyone would go to the trouble of using that particular phone box.

To frighten her? To make her believe that Derek really had come back from the dead to haunt her? No! She wouldn't believe that. Ghosts didn't make phone calls, Cam had said. And Cam was clever.

So, someone else was making the calls.

Her feet were leading her to Derek's grave. She had not been here since the funeral. Fresh flowers covered it still. Mum and Dad came up every Sunday. Maxine stood for a long time just staring at the headstone.

DEREK MOODY
BELOVED SON

There wasn't even a date. No one had been exactly sure when he had died. That had hurt Mum almost as much as anything else.

DEREK MOODY
BELOVED SON.

How true. Beloved. He was down there, and he was dead, and whoever was calling her was flesh and blood and alive and ... evil.

She closed her eyes and bent her head to pray.

She prayed that Derek would stay dead. Stay out of their lives. She wanted him gone.

The wind rustled through the trees, almost like a whisper. Like a whisper.

'Maxie ... Maxie ...'

She held her breath. It was her imagination. It had to be.

'Maxie.'

She half opened her eyes, peered through her lashes. All she could see was the trees.

And then, a movement. Was that a face? Half hidden, staring at her? A face she hardly recognised, yet knew so well?

No! No! It couldn't be. The voice was like the soft whisper of the trees.

'Come closer, Maxie. Don't be afraid. Come here. It's Derek.'

She wouldn't believe it. She wouldn't listen any more. She began to scream at the top of her voice. She screamed and screamed and suddenly ... everything went black.

CHAPTER ELEVEN

'Here, dearie, have some of this.'

There was a foul smell. Something disgusting was being poured down her throat. Maxine came to, coughing, spluttering, feeling sick.

'I didn't mean to frighten you, hen.'

The old man's hair was matted, his clothes shiny. He had grey stubble on his face and his breath reeked of stale wine. And he was trying to give her a drink from his bottle!

That realisation made her leap to her feet. What had happened. A bad dream? A nightmare?

The memory rushed back at her like a hurricane.

Derek in the trees. Derek's face. Derek's voice.

'NO!'

The old man jumped back at her yell. 'Now, don't go tellin' the police I scared you. I didn't even know you were there.' He was jabbing at her shoulder, trying to make her listen. But Maxine's eyes were searching frantically through the trees for some sign of whom or what she'd seen.

Nothing. There was nothing, no one there now.

At last she turned her gaze on the old man. She saw fear in his eyes too. Fear she might get him into trouble for being there.

'Did you see anyone else here?'

A puzzled frown creased his face. He was trying to understand what she meant.

'Did you see a boy. A young boy. There.' She gestured to the grave, the trees.

He put a finger to his lips thoughtfully. He might have been deliberating for *Who Wants to Be a Millionaire?* 'No,' he said finally. 'Nobody here but me and you.'

She pulled away from him and began to run. She had to get away from there. She had to think.

The old man called after her, 'Now, don't you go telling the police I scared you.'

She didn't even look back. He still shouted after her. But his tone changed. Not frightened any more, but disgusted.

'Oh, don't say thanks or anything. I wasted good drink on you!' His voice was getting fainter. 'See young people the day. No manners. You hear me? No blinkin' manners!'

She ran straight for home, not stopping. Too frightened to stop. Too frightened to think.

Mum was coming out of the kitchen as she raced in the front door. 'Maxine, you're home early.'

'So are you.' She hadn't expected anyone to be home. Mum should have been at work.

'I've taken a leave of absence,' Mum said with a shrug. And Maxine knew that was a lie. There was something else behind it. 'Why are you home?' Mum asked her.

'I don't feel well.' And that wasn't a lie. Maxine felt sick to her stomach.

Her mother frowned and came towards her. She felt her brow. 'Why, you're so hot, dear. You'd better go up and go straight to bed.' Suddenly, she began to sniff.

'What is that smell?' What 'that smell' was hit her like a ton of bricks. Her eyes went wide with alarm. 'Maxine! That's alcohol!'

That was all she needed, Maxine thought with a groan. Her parents to think she'd taken to drink.

'I know, Mum. I was running home so fast I bumped into an old drunk and he spilled his bottle all over me.'

It was too ridiculous to be anything else but the truth. Mum believed it anyway.

'Get into bed,' she said. 'I'll bring you up some tea.'

She began to walk into the kitchen, then she stopped at the door. 'I'm so glad to be home, Maxine,' she said dreamily. 'I feel Derek's presence here so strongly. He's here with us now.'

Yes! Maxine almost shouted at her. I've just brought him back from the cemetery! If she was being haunted by her brother, it was all her mother's fault. Her mother and that stupid fortune teller.

Dad came in at six and she could hear their murmured voices downstairs turn to anger. They've found out I wasn't at school, was her first thought. And she held her breath when he came into the bedroom minutes later. He looked troubled, his face tired and drawn.

'Did Mum tell you she'd lost her job?' he said at once.

So that was it? No leave of absence.

'But why? Mum's been there for ages.'

He shrugged. 'Her firm have been really good over the last year or so, very understanding. But maybe

82

having her son's ghost wandering about with her during working hours was too much for them to take.'

And too much for you, Dad. Maxine watched him and wondered how long it would be before Dad had had enough and moved out.

What was happening to her life? To all their lives? And all because of Derek. She hated him!

'So.' With a tired smile he turned his attention on her. 'How are you?'

'I just felt sick. I'm all right now.'

'You sure?' He touched his hand to her brow.

If only he meant it. If only she could tell him: 'I saw Derek at the graveside, Dad. I heard his voice.'

But no. It was impossible. He hadn't believed a disembodied voice on the phone. He would never believe this. He would accuse her of trying to get attention again.

'You know, about the other day. I'm sorry.' He tried for a real smile, but failed. 'I'm finding it hard to cope with your mother at the moment. But if you're getting phone calls from some sick crank, if they ever phone here again, you be sure to let me know. We'll let the police deal with it.'

And she could see then that he had so much to worry

him. How could she add to it? What if it hadn't been Derek in the cemetery? And of course it wasn't. It couldn't have been. She couldn't add to his troubles. Not now.

When she was alone again, she snuggled down in bed and tried to think. Whom could she tell? Who would understand? She had to tell someone. Father Matthew would listen. She could talk to him any time. But he didn't believe in ghosts. He would only think she was as dotty as her mother.

Could she tell Miss Ross? Miss Ross was sensible and down to earth, but this would be too much for even her to swallow.

That only left Cam. And she had a distinct feeling he didn't like her. But, and this was more important, he believed her. He didn't accuse her of making things up, or of hearing things. He took everything she said as the truth. Adults never did. No matter how well-intentioned they were.

She would tell Cam. He was clever. He would explain what was happening. She needed someone to explain it to her.

She left her bedside lamp on all night. In the dark she

was sure every shadow was Derek, every creak in the house his murmured voice.

'Don't think about it,' she kept telling herself. It must have been the old tramp she'd seen peering at her through the trees. It had been his voice she'd heard rasping at her. She almost convinced herself. It hadn't been Derek at all.

But in her dreams it was always Derek, shuffling about the graveyard like an old tramp, swigging wine in a derelict mausoleum.

Derek ... Derek ... Derek ...

CHAPTER TWELVE

Miss Ross was waiting for her next day at the school gates. Her face was grim.

'I covered for you yesterday, but I won't – I can't – do it again,' she said. Then her tone changed. It became softer, more gentle. 'I thought things would be different now that ...'

'Now that Derek's dead' were her unspoken words.

'But Derek's not dead.'

The teacher's pretty face puckered in a frown. 'Not dead? But of course he is, Maxine.'

'Not according to my mum,' Maxine said. She felt her eyes fill with tears and hated herself for it. Crying wouldn't help anything.

'Would you like me to come and have a word with her?'

Maxine thought about that. 'Are you going to tell her I wasn't at school yesterday?'

The teacher smiled. 'Not this time. But I would like to talk to her about how all this is affecting you.'

'She's lost her job!' Maxine blurted out. 'And I don't know how long my dad's going to put up with all of this. And she just won't let Derek go, and ...' Maxine had to force herself not to cry. But she wouldn't. The day was too sunny. The sky too blue. It was a day to be happy. She wouldn't let Derek spoil it for her.

'She's got me thinking I'm seeing him too.'

Big mistake! Maxine knew it at once. Her teacher's face froze. 'Don't even think that's possible, Maxine.'

Never tell an adult! Why had she forgotten that simple rule? They never understand. Never believe. 'It was my imagination,' she went on quickly. 'I was just so upset about the way Mum's been. It turned out to be an old drunk.'

Miss Ross looked worried. 'I think it's imperative I come and speak to your mum, Maxine. We can't have any more of this.'

'Please don't tell her I thought I saw him. Please.' Mum would be more likely to believe it than to think Maxine was going slightly potty too.

'Don't worry, Maxine,' Miss Ross said with a smile. 'You can trust me.'

Maxine didn't see Cam until lunchtime. He was standing at the tuck shop outside the school gates with Loui, the only other Chinese boy in the school. A boy who smiled almost as much as Cam didn't.

She was just about to go over to him when she saw Sweeney and his crowd sauntering over. Cam didn't even look up, his back was turned to them.

She wanted to call out, 'Look behind you!' But before she could say a word, Sweeney had begun to taunt Cam.

'Hey, slanty eyes, have you been chatting up my bird?'

Sweeney's 'bird' was Gale, a gum-chewing blonde, not exactly Cam's type.

Still Cam ignored him. Sweeney stepped closer. His cronies closed in around Cam and Loui. Loui looked nervous. By this time he had stopped smiling.

Maxine looked around. There were very few pupils there. Most were still in the canteen having lunch or back in their common rooms. Only a couple of the boys hovered round watching intently. They wouldn't interfere, she knew that. They would only watch, glad that Sweeney's wrath wasn't turned against them. There were four boys with Sweeney. Cam and Loui didn't stand a chance.

'Don't you ignore me, you Chinese turd!'

Still Cam kept his back turned.

Why didn't he just apologise? Maxine thought. For anything. Promise he would never do it again. There were only the two of them, and Loui was small and thin. Sweeney was built like a bulldog.

But Cam continued to ignore him. Kept his back turned as if Sweeney wasn't there. Loui wasn't quite so calm. Maxine watched him pull at his collar nervously. Sweeney noticed it too.

'You stay here with him and you're going to get the same.'

But Loui, despite his small size, held his ground beside Cam.

Sweeney cracked his knuckles. His gang were beginning to smile. This was going to be easy. So easy. Two slight Chinese boys against five of the biggest and toughest in the school.

Cam whispered something in Chinese to Loui, and Loui nodded and answered him. That really riled Sweeney. 'Hey, enough o' that stupid language. Can you not talk English?'

Only now did Cam turn his head to look at him. 'Better than you,' he said precisely.

Maxine gasped. What a thing to say to Sweeney! Was Cam crazy?

'Better than me!' Now Sweeney was really mad. Maxine felt like running in between them, trying to stop it. But her feet were like lead, and how could she help anyway? But she knew she would if it came down to it. She would run in there and do something.

'You've had it, China boy. You're for it.' And Sweeney moved threateningly closer.

'Five against two,' Cam said. 'Just the odds I like.'

Cam was potty, Maxine decided in that moment. What did he think he was playing at? He was only making things worse for himself. Sweeney turned to his gang. 'D'ye hear him! This guy deserves everything we're going to give him.'

He turned back to Cam. This was it. 'Get ready to die, China boy,' he threatened grimly.

And that was when it happened. Cam and Loui took a step back. They stood tall, their backs straight. They positioned their hands in an elegant, yet threatening gesture. A gesture she recognised, everyone did. Karate. They were going to use karate on Sweeney!

In a split second, Cam's leg shot out high in front of

him. Loui did the same. Cam yelled a cry of vengeance.

The whole thing took Sweeney and his gang by surprise. They'd expected to punch lumps out of Cam. Five against two. They hadn't expected to be confronted by a couple of Bruce Lees. Sweeney's cronies stepped back.

'Come on, then,' Cam said, and his leg shot out again. Sweeney stumbled back. He almost fell. 'Come on, then,' Cam said again.

The rest of the gang hesitated for only a moment, then one by one they deserted Sweeney. He looked around for them but they were gone. Now it was his turn to pull at his collar. Cam advanced towards him in one fluid movement. 'Just me and you, Sweeney,' he said.

'You'd like that, eh ...' Sweeney was moving back, step by frightened step. 'I don't know any karate.' He moved further back. 'You could kill me with one blow.'

Cam almost smiled. He nodded, and with a flick of his wrist his hand shot out towards Sweeney.

Sweeney was scared. And Sweeney didn't like being scared. He wouldn't forget this, nor Cam. There was real viciousness in his voice. 'I'll get you again, Cam. You're no' getting away with this, just remember that.

I'll get you when you don't expect it. And I'll make you sorry.'

And then he was gone, off and running after his mates.

Maxine leapt in the air. She couldn't help it. 'YES!' she yelled. Cam looked up at her. She went running and leaping towards him.

'Cam! That was brilliant. I didn't know you knew karate.'

Cam looked at Loui. Now the two of them laughed.

'We don't, Maxine. We just hoped it was a good way to frighten that lot off.'

That was even better. Maxine laughed so much she couldn't stop.

'He won't forget, you know,' Maxine warned him after Loui had left. 'You better watch, because he will get you.'

Cam looked as if he couldn't care less. That only annoyed her. He had an awful habit of annoying her. 'Anyway,' she said, 'you shouldn't be trying to steal his girlfriend. No wonder he was mad.'

Cam lifted an eyebrow. 'You can't think I'm interested in Gale. She's dumb. And talking of dumb females, what are you doing here?'

'You really are the most obnoxious ... I've got a good mind not to tell you why I came.'

He lifted an eyebrow. He knew she'd tell him. She was desperate to tell him.

Now that the moment had come to explain, she didn't know where to start. It all sounded so absurd. A phone call from the cemetery, a whispered voice by the graveside, a blurred face in the trees. But he listened, intently, and didn't look at her as if she was crazy. Didn't interrupt her with a disbelieving laugh.

'I did see him, Cam,' she insisted when she'd told him everything. 'I did hear his voice.'

He was silent for a long time. 'I do believe you, Maxine,' he said at last. And she was so relieved, as if she'd shared a burden. Someone else understood. 'We have three possibilities here.' He thought a moment longer. 'One. You saw a ghost. You are being haunted by your dead brother.'

That seemed the most logical to Maxine. She suddenly shouted, 'Brought back from the dead by that stupid fortune teller! I'm going to see her, Cam. I'm going to give her a piece of my mind!'

Cam ignored her. 'Two,' he went on, 'someone is deliberately trying to frighten you.'

That sounded even more logical. 'Someone cruel and vindictive. Do you think it could be Sweeney?'

But Sweeney didn't look a bit like Derek, and the face she'd seen in the trees had borne a resemblance to her brother. She was getting even more mixed up.

'What's the third possibility?'

'You're not going to like it,' he said.

She tutted. 'It couldn't be any worse than the other two. Go on, tell me. What's the third possibility?'

Cam's dark eyes never left hers. 'Has it ever occurred to you that Derek might not be dead at all? And that he really has come back?'

CHAPTER THIRTEEN

'But that's impossible! Stupid and impossible! Dad identified the body, remember? Of course it was Derek.'

Cam shrugged. 'Don't like to bring it up, but he had been dead a while. What was there to identify?'

'His clothes for a start!' she said angrily. 'The very clothes he went missing in. I won't listen to this.' She put her hands over her ears to shut out his voice. 'I'd rather it was a ghost. I'd rather it was a ghost!'

What he'd said upset her all day, and next day he was waiting at the school gates for her. She didn't want to talk to him. She ran and hid behind the bus shelters until he'd gone. Maxine knew she shouldn't blame him. She had asked him for advice. But – Derek not dead? That was impossible. Unthinkable.

She'd never believe it.

Home was miserable. The atmosphere was so thick with tension you could have cut it with the blunt edge of a ruler. They sat down to watch a video after tea and the tension was still there.

Once, watching a video had been one of Maxine's favourite family get-togethers. Mum would supply popcorn and choc ices and make a memory of it – one of Mum's favourite expressions. She used to have such a fund of them. 'Make today as good as it can possibly be and you've made a memory that can last for ever.' She hadn't made a memory, except painful ones, since Derek had gone.

The video was boring anyway. Some tripe about a man who pretends to be a doctor, takes over someone else's identity and ends up performing major surgery. What complete nonsense, Maxine thought. And she said so.

'How could he take out someone's appendix? He hasn't even been trained.'

'He learned from books,' Dad explained. 'During the war, you know, it wasn't always doctors who performed operations. Lots of people had to work on emergency cases, working from textbooks.'

'I don't believe it either,' Mum put in. 'I don't believe he could fool real doctors.'

'But it's a true story,' Dad insisted, as if he was talking to a couple of idiots.

In a way, Maxine thought, this was a bit like the old days. They could never watch a film without some kind of debate about it.

Dad began to explain. 'This man worked in a hospital for almost a year. No one suspected he was an impostor. It can happen. He behaved like a doctor. He looked like a doctor. Let's face it –' He began to laugh. 'I bet if I put a stethoscope around my neck and wore a white coat I could pass for a doctor.' He winked at Maxine and she giggled at the idea of it.

'Now you come to mention it,' Mum said thoughtfully. 'The last time I was at the doctor's I was giving this man all my symptoms, until he told me he was only painting the office.'

And suddenly they were all laughing, just as they used to in the old days.

It was an intrusion when the doorbell rang. Maxine didn't want to lose this feeling.

Dad switched off the video and Mum headed for the front door. A horrible, nightmarish thought struck Maxine. What if ... what if this boy who was pretending to be Derek was standing there on the doorstep? Derek, the way he had looked yesterday at the cemetery. Pale and drawn. Derek, and yet not Derek. She began to shiver. Mum couldn't take that! Maxine stood up. Her legs felt shaky.

'Maxine, are you all right? You're chalk white.'

'I don't feel too well.' She wanted to get to the front door before Mum, and already she knew it was too late. She could hear her mother turn the handle of the door.

'Maxine?' Her dad's voice came to her through a haze, as if from a million miles away. All she could hear clearly was her mother pulling open the front door.

'Maxine, sit down. You look about to faint!' Her dad pushed her into a seat.

She waited for her mother's scream.

'Miss Ross, how nice to see you.'

Maxine sank back in the chair with relief.

'I think we should get a doctor for Maxine,' Dad said as Miss Ross and Mum came into the living room. 'She almost fainted.'

Miss Ross looked at her. 'It's actually Maxine I've come to talk about.'

Maxine held her breath. She better not tell them she'd missed school again. She'd promised!

She didn't. 'Maxine's very worried about you, Mrs Moody.'

Mum said brightly. 'She needn't worry about me. I'm fine … now.'

Now that Derek is with her, she meant.

'We're both worried about her, Miss Ross. But you try telling her that,' Dad said. 'She has to let Derek go. No wonder Maxine's worried.'

'I won't let anyone take this away from me. Not my husband, not Maxine and certainly not you, Miss Ross.'

'No one wants to take it away. But it isn't healthy, and it isn't helping Maxine.'

Mum turned on Maxine angrily. 'So, do all your teachers know our business?' She didn't give Maxine time to answer her; instead she ranted on. 'Was this all planned? By both of you? What is this, gang-up-on-Mum night?'

Now Dad was angry. 'You have no right to say that, Gill.'

'I have no right!' Mum turned her fury on Miss Ross now. 'Does no one understand what I've been going through? I never believed Derek was …' She bit her lip, still refusing to say the word. 'And he was. Now, I know I have to come to terms with that. I've found a lifeline with this. Why does everyone want to snatch that life-line away from me?'

'Because it's unhealthy!' Dad shouted at her.

'Nonsense!'

'Gill, spiritualism is supposed to comfort you, but this isn't comforting you. This is taking over your life.'

'It hasn't taken over my life.'

Maxine jumped to her feet. 'It has, Mum. I might as well not be here!'

Mum looked at her as if she couldn't understand what she was saying. 'But Derek's here too,' she said at last. 'I know he is. And that comforts me.'

It was hopeless. She could never get through to her. 'No, he is not! He's not here. I've never understood why Derek ran away. But I do now. It was because he hated it here, almost as much as I do. I don't blame him for running away!'

CHAPTER FOURTEEN

Maxine ran to her room crying, knowing she'd hurt her mother and not caring. Miss Ross stayed on. She could hear her low, murmuring voice downstairs talking to Mum, comforting her.

But was that why Derek had run away? In spite of all her parents' efforts, Sweeney had never stopped tormenting him. And when he had begun to fight back, he'd been classed as the troublemaker. Their parent's sympathy for Derek had turned to anger as he got into more trouble. Had he done all that to get their attention, just as Maxine was doing? And when even that hadn't worked, had he gone? She had hated him then. Hated the hurt he was causing her mum and dad. Yet she could still remember times when Derek would come into her room and spend hours helping her with homework or showing new ways to work on his computer. So which one was the real Derek?

She tried to remember now the day he left. An ordinary breakfast, or so it had seemed at the time. Yet he'd been shouting at her, calling her names. She had tried to punch him and she'd fallen off the stool. Mum had comforted her, been annoyed at Derek.

'What's wrong with you this morning?' she had shouted, not waiting for an answer. 'You're even worse than usual. I'm so sick of this, Derek!'

'No one ever listens!' he had yelled at her. 'Why don't any of you ever listen to me?'

How often had Maxine thought that too?

And Derek had grabbed his rucksack and gone. That was the last she had ever seen of him. His last look at her had been an angry glare. Her last gesture had been to stick out her tongue at him in defiance. The last words his mother had spoken to him had been a threat. 'Your dad and I are going to have to speak to you about your behaviour.'

No wonder her mother grieved so much for him. It was guilt. Guilt that perhaps that threat had been the last straw. Derek hadn't come home, and now he never would.

Did Mum really blame herself for his going? Or, even

worse – did she blame Maxine? That would account for a lot of things.

There was a soft tapping on the bedrom door. 'Maxine, can I come in?' It was Miss Ross, and now it was Maxine's turn to be comforted.

'How are you?' she asked gently, sitting on the bed.

'Is Mum okay?' That was all Maxine wanted to know.

'I've had a word with her. I know it's hard for you. But you have to be very grown-up about this. Give her a little more time. Derek's dead, and she's doing her best to come to terms with with it.' Miss Ross touched her hand, squeezed it. 'There's something you're not telling me. I'm here to help you. You must trust me.'

Miss Ross would know what to do. She needed someone sensible, like Miss Ross. Miss Ross liked her, whereas she wasn't sure that Cam did. Oh, she was so mixed up!

'You'll think I'm crazy. It sounds crazy.'

Miss Ross moved closer to her, intrigued. 'Tell me, Maxine.'

Maxine sighed. 'Things have happened. Things I don't understand. Strange things ...'

It was right at that moment the door opened and Dad

103

came in. He noted the glance that passed between them both. 'Am I interrupting something? Girl talk, eh? Will I go?'

He was trying to be light-hearted, but Maxine could tell he needed to talk just as much as she had. 'No, Dad, come in.'

Miss Ross couldn't quite hide her disappointment. She stood up, reluctant to go. Maxine could understand that. She hated it when, just at the most exciting part of a programme, there was a commercial break. Or at an edge-of-your-seat part of a story, the end of a chapter. This was a commercial break.

'Maybe I could come and see you in the morning?' Maxine said softly.

Miss Ross smiled and patted her hand. 'Yes. You can talk to me in the morning.'

'I'll see Miss Ross out,' Dad said, 'and then ...'

Maxine leapt out of bed. She felt better already. 'I'll go downstairs. Maybe we can even finish watching that rotten video.'

Mum had gone to bed. They were alone. They didn't talk. But for that one night she felt closer to Dad than she had done for a long time.

Mum didn't appear for breakfast next morning, and Dad didn't comment on that. He went off to work with a promise from Maxine that she wouldn't dawdle or be late for school.

Maxine had no intention of dawdling. She was looking forward to seeing Miss Ross and getting all of this off her chest.

Dad had gone and Maxine was just about to leave when the phone rang. She stopped for a moment, holding the front door open, wondering whether to answer it or not. Her curiosity won, and she lifted the receiver. She was ready to shout, to scream if it was that husky, whispered voice again. But she didn't get the chance.

'Maxie, don't hang up please! You have to meet me. You have to let me explain. Meet me. Please. In St Jude's after school. I know you go there. I've watched you.' There was a sudden, sharp intake of breath. 'Someone's coming. I have to go. Don't tell anyone. Anyone! Promise.'

And the line went dead.

CHAPTER FIFTEEN

She didn't believe it. She wouldn't believe it. She wanted to cry out, to call Mum. Ask her what to do. But Mum was still in bed. She was upset, and this would only upset her more. It was a hoax. It had to be. Ghosts don't make phone calls. She had to hang on to that.

No. This was no ghost. And it wasn't Derek. Derek was dead and buried and he would never come back. Dad had identified the body. She'd been to the funeral. She'd even cried.

No. This wasn't Derek. Alive or dead, even Derek could never be this mean.

This was someone who hated her. Who was trying to frighten her with this cruel trick? Sweeney? Sweeney and cruelty went together.

But whoever was doing this wanted to meet her in the church. Would Sweeney risk entering the house of

God? She didn't think so. Somehow she was sure that Sweeney, like Dracula, would dissolve if he ever ventured inside a church. But whoever it was knew she went there. He'd watched her – hadn't she always felt someone was watching her? Well, she would meet him. In fact, once she'd made the decision, she couldn't wait to meet him. And when she did ... she would have a surprise ready for him. He was going to be really sorry he'd ever tried to trick Maxine Moody.

Miss Ross was waiting for her when she came out of the history class. Maxine had almost forgotten her promise to tell her everything. There was so much more to tell now.

'Don't tell anyone,' he had pleaded.

Whoever it was wanted to get her on her own, to frighten her. He thought she'd be walking into a trap, but she would have a little surprise up her sleeve.

'We can talk in the staffroom.' Miss Ross was ushering her in with a smile.

She could trust Miss Ross. However (all these thought tumbled through her head in a millionth of a second), if she told her about the latest phone call, she'd try to stop her meeting in the church. She'd point out the dangers. Or want to go with her. No.

This was something she was going to handle on her own.

'I really don't have time this morning, Miss Ross,' she said, trying to dodge past her.

Miss Ross looked puzzled. 'You have a free period right now. I checked.' She took her by the elbow, gently but firmly. 'Come on. Into the staffroom. I'll make you some tea.'

'I really can't this morning.' She searched her mind for some reason, couldn't think of any.

'I think you need to talk about this, Maxine.' Miss Ross gave her a gentle push towards the open staffroom door.

Just then Maxine caught sight of Cam coming out of one of the classrooms. 'I promised I'd meet Cam.' She started to wave frantically at him, trying to catch his attention. Please, don't ignore me, she prayed.

'Cam! Cam! Over here.'

Cam looked up, as baffled as Miss Ross. 'Me?'

Maxine pulled herself free of her teacher. 'I'll have to go.'

Miss Ross frowned. 'I don't understand you, Maxine.'

She so wanted her to understand. 'Give me a couple

of days, Miss Ross, then maybe I'll really have something to tell you.'

She began to hurry down the corridor towards Cam. Miss Ross called after her, 'You're up to something, Maxine. What is it?'

She pretended not to hear, and almost knocked Cam off his feet. 'What on earth's got into you?'

She began to giggle. 'Miss Ross is now convinced you're my boyfriend.'

Cam looked horrified. He stuck two fingers down his throat and pretended to be sick.

'Ha! You should be so lucky!' Maxine said. Miss Ross still stood outside the staffroom watching them both with interest.

Maxine waved at her, and muttered out of the side of her mouth, 'Look as if you're asking me out for a date.'

Cam started to laugh. Maxine was quite annoyed, and amazed. She'd never seen Cam laugh before. 'I don't see what's so funny,' she said. However, something convinced Miss Ross, for with a shrug of her shoulders she disappeared into the staffroom.

'I mean, asking *you* for a date? Come on! I'd have to be desperate.'

Maxine stamped on his feet and began to walk away.

'See you, Cam. You can be really insulting at times.'

He followed her, still laughing. 'Come on, Maxine, I wanted to talk to you anyway. To apologise.'

Maxine could hardly believe her ears. 'What? You apologise to me?'

Cam shrugged. 'Yes, you asked me to help you, and I wasn't much help, was I? I'm sorry.'

'No, you were not. But it's all right now,' Maxine said calmly. 'I know someone is playing tricks on me.'

Something in her tone made Cam immediately suspicious. 'Has something happened?'

She longed to tell him. He was the one person she could tell. But she knew what would happen if she did. He – like Miss Ross – would take over the whole thing. He was a boy, after all, and older than she was. That was what he would say. That she shouldn't go alone. That she shouldn't go at all.

No way!

She wanted to tell him, but she wouldn't. Not this time. Not until it was all over. She would be able to tell him who it was who had been making those phone calls.

'Something *has* happened,' he said, knowing by her hesitation it was true. 'Another phone call? Have you seen him again?'

She started to run off down the corridor. 'Phone me tonight, Cam. I'll have something to tell you. I promise.'

And she would have something to tell him. Because today, after school, she was going to meet the mysterious boy who was pretending to be Derek.

CHAPTER SIXTEEN

St Judes's was empty when she went in, its side altars dark and gloomy. There was something comforting about a church in the afternoon. She closed the door quietly behind her and stood for a moment listening to the muted sounds of the traffic outside. She could be a million miles from everything in here. It was so quiet. The only sound she could hear inside was the sound of her own breathing.

Well, she was here. But was anyone else?

Her footsteps clattered on the tiled floor, echoing up into the high roof. A shaft of sunlight suddenly shone through the stained-glass window and sent myriad colours all around the church. Then a cloud obscured the sun again and the church seemed darker than ever.

Maxine knelt by the glowing candles at St Anthony's altar. There was no one here in the church. She was sure of it. Perhaps she had been a fool to come. She glanced at her watch. She would wait ten minutes, she decided, and if no one had come by then, she would go.

She looked up at the face of St Anthony. The flickering flames made the statue seem almost alive, his eyes watching her. Even blinking now and then. She wasn't afraid of him, standing there in his alcove, cradling the Baby Jesus. He'd always been her favourite.

Suddenly the west door opened and Maxine caught her breath. A band of light streamed into the church and someone entered. She couldn't see who it was because a stone pillar blocked her view. Clip, clip, clip. Footsteps heading down the side aisle. Any second now whoever those footsteps belonged to would come into her sight. Maxine tensed.

It was an old lady, clipping towards the Lady altar. Maxine felt the relief flood over her. The newcomer caught sight of the young girl in school uniform kneeling in front of St Anthony and her old eyes smiled approvingly. Maxine watched her closely, half expecting her to throw off her disguise and become ... who? Master criminals were always doing things like that in books.

The old woman reached in her pocket; coins jingled

and then tinkled into the box before she reached for a candle. If she was one of those old ladies who took hours to say a rosary, Maxine's visit would be a waste of time. No one was going to appear while she was there.

But the woman knelt only for a few moments, then struggled to her feet again. She turned to Maxine with another smile and a nod, then began to clip-clip back up the aisle.

Maxine glanced again at her watch. The ten minutes had passed surprisingly quickly. Just a couple of minutes more and then, no matter what, she was off. She was hanging around in this quiet, empty church not a moment longer.

Yet something had changed. For a minute Maxine couldn't think what it was. She looked all around but saw nothing, no movement. Then she held her breath and realised at once what it was.

Someone was breathing, softly and steadily, close by.

She was not alone in there any more.

Where had he come from? Surely she would have heard someone enter, unless that someone really was a ghost! NO! She pushed that thought away. She would not be afraid. She was there to have this thing settled once and for all.

'OK, where are you?' she demanded, and her voice echoed up into the highest rafters.

For a moment there was no answer, just that slow, steady breathing somewhere close.

Then – 'I'm here, Maxie.' The voice was no more than a whisper. It seemed to come from St Anthony himself. She gasped and looked up at the flickering eyes.

'I'm here, in the alcove.' She peered, but it was dark behind the statue and all she could make out was a vague shape, a shadow undefined.

She slipped her hand into her pocket. She was ready for anything. 'Come out, let me see you. I've had enough of your silly games.'

'This isn't a silly game. I'm your brother. You must believe me.'

Now that he had said it, she believed it even less. 'No, you're not! Derek's dead. Dead and buried up in the graveyard.'

'No. That's a boy I changed clothes with one day. We laughed because he looked so much like me in my clothes.' He seemed almost to be talking to himself. 'So long ago ... I can hardly remember. How can I make you believe me?'

'By coming out of the shadows, by coming home. By stepping out into the light. Let me touch you. Let me see you. You're not Derek! You can't be!'

'You don't know what it's like to see your own name on a gravestone. To see the story of your death in a newspaper.' The whisper suddenly became a heart-breaking plea. 'I don't want to be dead, Maxie,' the voice whispered. 'That's why I came back. I had to let you know.'

'What do you care what we think? You just went off and didn't care how much it hurt Mum and Dad. You only care about yourself. Mum's almost crazy with grief. And you say you're here. Alive. And you still won't come home. And you wonder why I don't believe you!' With that, she realised herself why she didn't believe him. It struck her like a thunderbolt. 'I know you're not Derek. Because Derek could never be as cruel as that.'

There was desperation in the voice when it spoke again. 'I can't come home. It would just all start again.'

'I won't believe anything till I see your face. Touch you. I won't believe you're my brother. You're just someone wicked who wants to frighten me.'

There was a long sigh. 'You want to see me ... OK, you can see me ...'

Right at that second the vestry door was being pulled open. Someone was coming, alerted by her shouting.

Suddenly, St Anthony began to move. He began to topple towards her. She let out a scream. This was it! He was coming to get her. Well, she was ready for him. She reached back into her pocket and gripped the alarm and set it off. The alarm she had taken from her mother's handbag in case of emergency. And this was definitely an emergency.

A screeching whistle rent the air. Maxine stumbled back, her scream almost as loud as the alarm. St Anthony was hurtling towards her. The great statue that stood taller than herself was zooming closer. He was going to fall on her!

And then she was being dragged from its path, just as the statue crashed to the tiled floor and the alabaster saint exploded into pieces and sent debris and dust everywhere.

'Maxine! Are you all right? What happened?'

It was Father Matthew.

'I don't know, Father.'

He took the alarm from her and switched it off.

'It just fell, Father. I never touched it. Honest.'

'Of course you didn't.' He was studying the alarm,

puzzled she should have such a thing. 'Was anyone else here?'

'Why? Did you see anybody else?' She said it too quickly. He looked at her, suspicion in his eyes.

'I heard you shouting. Who were you shouting at?'

She had to think quickly, and she did. 'Him!' She pointed to what was left of St Anthony. 'I've always prayed to him and he's let me down. He probably jumped on me deliberately to get his own back.'

Father Matthew managed a smile. 'I don't think St Anthony would ever do that. It was just an accident.' He helped her into a pew. 'You sit here. I'll go and get my car keys. I'm taking you home.'

'I'll help clear this up,' she offered, but Father Matthew was insistent.

'I'll be back in a minute,' he said, hurrying back into the vestry.

As she waited, Maxine realised she was shaking. She wanted to cry. The statue of St Anthony lay shattered at her feet. It might have killed her. Had he pushed it deliberately? And who was *he*? There was no one in the alcove now. Where had he gone? She hadn't heard him leaving, nor seen him. Was it a ghost? Derek's ghost? She was frightened and too confused to think anything through properly right now. She needed time to sort out her thoughts.

All at once, the sun illuminated the church and in the sudden light something shining among the debris caught Maxine's eye. She couldn't quite make out what it was. She got up from her seat and bent to pick it up. It was a long gold chain with a St Christopher medal attached.

She knew before she looked at the inscription exactly what it would say.

DEREK MOODY

CHAPTER SEVENTEEN

Her mother's first reaction when she came in the door with Father Matthew was, 'What's she done now?'

Maxine had wanted to run to her. She wanted her mother to reassure her that the medal she had in her pocket couldn't be Derek's. That it couldn't have been Derek in the church. That Derek was dead, gone for ever.

Instead, there was her mother's long-suffering frown to deal with and her annoyed question.

'She's done nothing, Mrs Moody,' Father Matthew said quickly, adding, 'in fact, she was being very good. Putting up a candle to St Anthony.'

Oh boy, if only he knew!

Her father came from the kitchen, glasses perched on his nose, a chicken under his arm. He looked so funny, Maxine wanted to laugh.

'Something must have happened,' he said. 'Why have you brought Maxine home?'

'She got a bit of a scare. I'm afraid St Anthony wasn't very grateful for that candle.' He gave a little laugh. Priestly attempt at humour, Maxine thought. He should never try it. 'He almost toppled on top of her.'

Mum went chalk white and lowered herself gently into a chair. Maybe she does care. That thought made everything seem worthwhile. It only lasted for a second, however.

'I wasn't hurt, Mum, honestly.'

Mum was shaking her head. 'You were praying for Derek.' She didn't ask. She was telling her. 'And the statue fell. Don't you see, it must mean something.'

'Yes. It means I was almost flattened.' She knew she sounded cheeky. Didn't care.

Dad sat down too and began pointing the chicken at his wife. 'It means nothing. And don't try to make something of it.'

Father Matthew agreed. 'It was just an unfortunate accident. That was all.'

Her father looked at her. 'You didn't touch the statue, did you? Push it or anything?'

She felt he wanted her to say she had. That it was all

her fault. Like everything else. Well, she wasn't taking the blame for this. 'No. I didn't.'

'I thought for a minute there was someone else there.' Father Matthew's eyes bored into her. 'But Maxine says there wasn't.'

'There wasn't! Why would I lie?' Her dad's eyebrows shot up. She wasn't supposed to speak to a priest like that. He glanced at Father Matthew and the priest shrugged.

'It was simply an accident, Mrs Moody. I've always said he wasn't secured.' Was that a wee lie, she wondered, to make everything better?

Mum was looking at him, but she wasn't seeing him. She was thinking of someone else entirely. There are no such things as accidents. Everything has a reason. A purpose. Mum was remembering that. Believing it.

Father Matthew was offered tea, but declined. He had an early-evening mass at the local prison.

'Perhaps Maxine could see me to my car?' He wanted to talk to her. It didn't matter that she didn't want to talk to him.

'I know it looks as if they're blaming you,' he said once they were outside.

'They always do.'

'They're not. Not really. Not deep down. You're only thirteen, Maxine, and you have to be so grown-up right now. Your mum and dad are hurting. Your dad is trying to understand your mother's behaviour and to help her. If they're neglecting you, it's only for this short while. This will pass, and you'll be a happy family again.'

How she wished she could believe that! A happy family again – it seemed an impossible dream at the moment.

'I just want you to tell me one thing, Maxine.' He hesitated, searching for the right words. 'I don't mind if you lied to me before, and I think you did.' Maxine couldn't stop her blush. 'But I'd like the truth now. Someone else was in the church.' He stared at her, with blue eyes that seemed to reach right down to her soul. 'Who was it, Maxine?'

She swallowed and tried to look away from that hypnotic gaze. 'You won't get anyone into trouble. It was an accident. I just want to know who was with you. Was it someone you were afraid of?'

'What makes you think that, Father?'

'You did have an alarm in your pocket. What made you set it off?'

She stumbled over her words. 'The s-statue falling. I got a fright.'

He waited a moment. Maxine said nothing. 'I don't understand why you can't tell me.'

How much would he understand? Could she tell him? He was a priest after all. She fingered the chain in her pocket nervously. Father Matthew waited for her answer.

What was the point of telling him? She wouldn't even know where to begin. It was all too complicated. So she said nothing. Finally she lowered her gaze away from his.

He didn't seem hurt or angry. Just puzzled. He got into his car and rolled down the window. 'When you're ready to talk, Maxine, I'm here. Trust me.' Then he drove off.

Nothing much was said about the incident over dinner. It had been too late to cook the chicken, so they had something instead from the freezer. Mum was in a world of her own, and before dessert rose silently and went into the living room. Dad's eyes followed her.

'And this has only made things worse,' he said.

Maxine slammed down her fork. She had been

waiting for a comment like that. 'I didn't do it on purpose.'

'I know. I know.' Dad reached across the table and clutched her hand. 'I'm sorry, Maxine.' He sat silent for a moment. 'I just can't reach your mother any more. She needs professional help.'

Maxine began to be afraid. 'What do you mean, Dad? Do you think she's ... crazy?'

'Of course not,' he said at once. 'Mum's been through a lot. She has to let go of the past. I can't seem to help her do that. A professional might.'

At least she wasn't getting phone calls, nor was she hearing voices in churches. At that second Maxine would have given anything to confide in her dad, but that would only make things a hundred times worse.

But there was one thing she could ask and not give rise to any suspicion.

'Did you get any of Derek's belongings back?'

He seemed puzzled by the question. 'Not his clothes, if that's what you mean.'

'No. I meant his St Christopher medal. The one I gave him for his birthday.' She waved towards the photograph on the hall table. 'I've been meaning to ask you if you got it back.'

'No. He was living rough, remember. The police said his gold chain would have been the first thing he would have sold to buy food.'

'You think he sold it to someone?'

'Or someone stole it. That's probably more likely.' He squeezed her hand. 'I'm so sorry. It would have been a nice keepsake for you. But I'm afraid we've seen the last of Derek's St Christopher medal.'

CHAPTER EIGHTEEN

Cam phoned at seven o'clock. She'd almost forgotten him. So much had happened to her that day. It was impossible to talk to him on the phone so they arranged to meet at Simmy's arcade.

'I'm just going out, Dad,' she called into the kitchen. Her reason was all ready, hanging on her lips. Four of the girls in her class getting together for a class project. 'Whose house?' he would ask, and she would answer, 'We'll meet, then decide. I'll call, don't worry.'

It all sounded plausible and reasonable and meant they couldn't phone to check up on her. 'Did you hear me, Dad? I'm going out.'

Dad appeared at the kitchen door. 'Fine,' was all he said. 'Don't be late.'

So much for her excuse. She might have known. It

didn't matter where she was going. They didn't care any more.

Cam was challenging the Mighty Zola once again when she went into the arcade. And winning. His name appeared at the very top of the list of Mighty Champions. By now, Mighty Maxie had been totally obliterated.

What was she confiding in this smart alec for? And of course, that was precisely the answer. Because he was this smart alec.

'OK, what happened that was so mysterious you couldn't tell me on the phone?'

She pulled him away from the Mighty Zola and in a quiet corner told him everything that had happened. His expression didn't change. Even when she described in graphic detail (adding some bits to make it more exciting) how the statue had almost crushed her. Did nothing surprise him? Shock him? Frighten him?

Finally, she drew the medal from her pocket and showed it to him.

He took it from her, wound the chain through his fingers and held the medal in the palm of his hand. 'This is definitely Derek's?'

'I should know. I bought it for him.'

He studied it for so long that Maxine grew impatient. 'And don't say ghosts don't leave presents. I know that. This was no ghost.'

Still he said nothing.

'Well, don't you see what this means? Derek must be alive.' She went on when he still didn't answer her. 'I don't know how, but he must be alive.'

'You didn't actually see him.'

'I saw someone.'

'But you couldn't swear it was Derek.'

'It was Derek, it had to be. The medal!'

'Why couldn't he just step out into the light and let you see him? That would have convinced you. The church was empty. There was no danger there.'

And suddenly it occurred to her that perhaps the church hadn't been empty. Had Father Matthew been somewhere in the shadows, listening to their murmured voices? Standing stealthily behind the vestry door? She said all of this to Cam.

His explanation was more simple. 'Father Matthew probably thinks you're potty, standing in front of a statue talking to yourself.'

She stomped away from him in a huff. He hurried after her. 'I'm trying to be logical.'

'Oh, Mr Spock returns! You were the one who suggested Derek might still be alive in the first place. There are three possibilities, you said.' She mimicked him in a singsong voice. 'One. Someone is playing a trick on me. Two. Derek is a ghost ... oh, but I forgot, ghosts don't make telephone calls. Scrub that one. And there is a third. Derek is alive and well and living behind St Anthony's statue! Well, he is. The medal proves it. Smart alec!'

She sounded childish. She knew it and blushed to her roots.

Cam didn't seem to notice. 'Now I think there could be another possibility.'

For the life of her Maxine couldn't think what that might be. 'And what is that?' she asked.

'Derek was gone for a long time. You don't know the kind of people he might have met. Not very nice people. Perhaps he told someone all about his family, and that person stole his medal, and now that Derek's dead he's come to make you think he's Derek. And someone like that would be dangerous.' He hesitated. 'The question is, Maxine, did the statue fall ... or was it pushed?'

CHAPTER NINETEEN

'I think you've got to accept the possibility that you're dealing with someone dangerous here. I think it's time you told the police what's been happening.'

The notion appalled her. 'The police! You've got to be kidding! And tell them what? I had a phone call from my dead brother. Then he tried to assault me with a statue. They'll have me carted off to the funny farm.'

'You have to tell someone. It's not fair, carrying this on your own.'

'Not my parents,' she said, imagining the scene – telling her mother, watching her face light up with hope. Derek was alive! Then crumple into despair again. Worse despair when the truth dawned. No, she couldn't put her through that. 'I couldn't do that, Cam. Mum's on the verge of a nervous breakdown. I heard Dad say that to Father Matthew. This could send her right over the edge. And my dad too, if it goes on much longer. He'll go and not come back, just like Derek.'

'I thought you didn't care about them.'

He must be able to see the tears in her eyes. She wouldn't let *him* see her cry. She sniffed them away.

'You know, Maxine,' he went on in a surprised tone, 'you really are a nice person.'

'Are you trying to be funny?' she snapped.

Cam took a step back. 'It was meant to be a compliment. It surprises me as much as it surprises you.'

'You really are the most horrible person I've ever come across!'

'And you are the strangest little girl I've ever met.'

He was staring at her as if she was an alien species in a laboratory. That was it. An alien species. 'Don't you dare call me a little girl! I'm almost fourteen.'

'And you act it.'

That was the last straw. She stomped away from him angrily. He really knew how to get her back up. 'I don't know why I keep talking to you.'

She ran all the way home, until she reached her own tree-lined street. There, she slowed down and realised with a shiver how dark the night was. If Cam was right, someone meant her harm. Someone who seemed to know her every move.

The only sound as she hurried up the street was her own footsteps. She jumped at the plaintive hoot of an owl and every rustle in the trees made her start.

No one suddenly stepped out from behind a tree. No one leapt at her from the bushes. But all the way she could feel eyes watching her. Her imagination? No. She wouldn't believe that any more. Too much had happened. Someone *was* watching her. She paused at the front door and looked up and down the street. It was empty. Only a cat scurrying across the road disturbed the quiet. Yet she was was sure. Someone was out there, watching.

Over the next few days it grew increasingly difficult to avoid Miss Ross. She would try to catch up with her in corridors or wait for her on the playground. Maxine watched for her all the time, and managed to miss her.

One she didn't miss was Sweeney. She was peering out of a corridor window, watching for Miss Ross at the school gates, when she was suddenly pushed from behind.

'Here, it's wee Maxie.' She turned to find him standing in front of her. His ugly grey face was sneering at her as usual. 'And getting weer every time I see 'er.' He laughed at his feeble joke. So did his cronies. They would be terrified not to.

'At least I'll grow. But you're ugly and there's no chance of you growing out of that.'

He brought his face down close to hers. 'I can always get plastic surgery.'

Maxine sneered back. 'There ain't that much plastic in the world, pal.'

Sweeney stood straight. His face reddened. He couldn't think of an answer and knew that little Maxine Moody had won a round. He didn't like that one bit.

'You're getting a bit too cheeky for your own good,' he spat at her. 'Maybe it's time you got some of what your brother got.'

'Or maybe I'm getting it already,' she snapped at him. 'It's you that's behind this. You're trying to frighten me, aren't you? Well, you won't. I won't let you.' She didn't wait for an answer. 'I'm not scared of you, Sweeney.' The truth was she was terrified of him. But at that moment her anger overcame any fear she might have. 'You never gave my brother any peace when he was alive. But now he's dead, you better let him rest.'

Just then, Cam appeared from nowhere. He grabbed Maxine and pushed her in front of him down the corridor away from Sweeney.

Sweeney did nothing to stop him, afraid that Cam might let go with another karate kick. He shouted after him, 'Aye, get her away from me. She'll be sorry one of these days! And as for you, China boy, I'll get around to you soon.'

Cam ignored him. 'Are you so stupid, Maxine? You're taunting him.' He mimicked her. '"There ain't that much plastic in the world." Imagine saying something like that to Sweeney.' Then he laughed. He actually laughed! 'It was a good one, though.'

'It's because of him all this has happened, Cam. Everything that's happened to Derek, to my family, is his fault. It all began with him. I wish I could do something to pay him back!'

'Don't let him bother you,' Cam said slowly. 'It's the best way to pay him back. He can't handle that. Sweeney's nothing, Maxine. And he's never going to be anything. Forget him.'

Something was stirring in her memory. What was it? Cam saw her puzzled expression. 'Is anything wrong, Maxine?'

Right at that second it hit her, and the memory made her shiver. 'Did you hear what he called me, Cam? Sweeney called me Maxie. No one ever called me Maxie but Derek. It must be Sweeney that's behind this, Cam. It has to be!'

CHAPTER TWENTY

Mum was on a high when Maxine went home. Obviously she'd had another session with Luella Oribine.

She had a 'no one is going to take this feeling away from me' kind of look about her. Defiant. Daring Maxine or Dad to say a word. Dad picked at his dinner, pushing food around the plate with his fork.

Just watching the two of them convinced Maxine she was right. She couldn't tell them anything.

She lay in bed that night, fingering Derek's chain. Was Cam right? Had someone stolen it from him? And was that the someone who was terrorising her now? Or was it really Sweeney? Had he stolen the chain from Derek before Derek had gone? She wished she could remember if he was wearing it that day. I bet this chain could solve the whole mystery if it could only speak, she thought.

The bedroom door opened and Mum came in. Maxine thrust the chain under her pillow hurriedly. Mum mustn't see it.

'I came in to say goodnight and to apologise.' She sat on the edge of the bed and stroked Maxine's hair. It had been so long since she'd done anything like that, it took Maxine by surprise. She shrank back.

'I understand, Maxine. No wonder you don't trust me. I've neglected you. I've been so wrapped up in my own problems, I've not thought about yours.'

Maxine was sure her mouth was hanging open. Couldn't help it. What had brought on this sudden concern? Mum's next words told her.

'Derek said I've to take care of you.'

Maxine shivered.

'I know you find it hard to understand, but it comforts me. Makes me feel better.' Her mother ruffled her hair. 'If you all just give me time, I'm going to be better.'

You're going to be better, Mum, Maxine thought, as she watched her leave the room. But you're not going to let Derek go, ever.

She began to get angry. What right had Derek to come back from wherever he was and interfere in their lives? He should have enough to do learning to play a harp! She had a good mind to go and tell that fortune teller off. And that was when it struck her: if Derek was passing messages back and forth like the Royal Mail, why couldn't he pass one on to her? Why couldn't he tell her exactly what was happening? She was going to see Mrs Luella Oribine. She was going to ask Derek himself.

At three thirty next day, instead of going home, Maxine turned in the direction of Mrs Oribine's house. Mum kept her address handy, stuck on the fridge door. Luella Oribine lived on one of the new estates on the edge of town. A neat expanse of bungalows and tidy gardens. Mrs Oribine's was easy to spot. It looked exactly like her. The garden was a mass of vibrant colours, yellow marigolds, red tulips, tall lilac lupins. Maxine rang the doorbell and waited on the steps for the front door to be opened. Finally it was answered by Mrs Oribine herself.

Did this woman never try to look the part, Maxine wondered? Had she no pride? She was a fortune teller, for goodness sake, yet there wasn't a gold earring in sight. Instead, she stood there, her unruly hair tied up in a multicoloured scarf, a cigarette dangling from her lips. She was clutching a tin of polish and a yellow duster.

She stared at Maxine, obviously not recognising her. Then she took a step past her and looked up and down the street. Maxine followed her gaze, up and down, wondering what she was looking for.

Finally, Luella Oribine said in a sharp voice, 'Don't want any.'

The woman was dotty, Maxine decided.

'Want any what?' Maxine asked her. Already, Mrs Oribine was back inside the house getting ready to close the door in Maxine's face. 'I'm not selling anything.' Then she added quickly, keeping a wary eye on that closing door, 'Don't you recognise me, Mrs Oribine?'

The fortune teller peered closer. Maxine couldn't take her eyes off that cigarette ash, amazed it still hadn't dropped to the ground.

'Of course, you're the wee lassie, Moody, aren't you? I thought you were one of them kids selling macaroons.' She looked suddenly concerned. 'How's your mother?'

Almost as dotty as you, Mrs Oribine, Maxine could have answered. Instead she simply shrugged.

'What brings you here?' She could speak with the

cigarette still in her mouth, and the ash still attached precariously. Maxine was fascinated.

'Mum gets messages. That's all she talks about.' As Maxine spoke, a guilty flush passed over Mrs Oribine's face.

'Oh, dear,' she said.

'I want a message too,' Maxine said, getting to the point straight away. 'I want to talk to him.'

At last Mrs Oribine took the cigarette from her mouth. 'I hoped this wouldn't happen.'

'Don't tell me I'm too young to get a message.' Maxine was determined not to be put off. 'It's important. I must. You've got to let me talk to him.'

If she said 'oh, dear' again, Maxine was sure she would scream.

'I think you'd better come in, hen,' she said. 'There's something I think I should tell you.'

CHAPTER TWENTY-ONE

Mrs Oribine's kitchen was sparkling clean and very modern. However, it looked as if she'd had three different designers in to put it all together. All white and chrome on one side, panelled wood on another and bright red worktops on a third.

She ushered Maxine to a seat at the table. 'Do you want something to drink, hen?'

Maxine shook her head. 'What did you mean? There's something you should have told me?'

Mrs Oribine sat down across from Maxine and immediately began to light up another cigarette. Maxine coughed theatrically, but she didn't seem to notice. In fact, the first thing she did was blow smoke right into Maxine's face.

'When I came to your house that first time, hen, I could see how desperate your mother was. She wanted so much to hear from her son. Some kind of message, anything. And I thought ... where was the harm if it was going to comfort her?'

Maxine shot to her feet. 'You mean you didn't receive any message from Derek?'

'Nothing. Not even the feeling he was trying to get through.'

'That's disgusting. You lied!' Maxine couldn't keep the anger out of her voice.

Luella Oribine pulled her back into the chair. 'I want you to know I've never done anything like that before. I'm a very reputable medium. It's against every principle I have.' She took a long pull at her cigarette. 'I did it with the best intentions. You must believe that.'

'No message at all?'

She was shaking her head. 'I never had any psychic connection with your brother.'

'You're a ... phoney?'

Mrs Oribine almost swallowed her cigarette, and now she shot to her feet and began pacing up and down the kitchen. 'Me? A phoney! I'll have you know, young lady, I am a respected medium, renowned the length and breadth of the country.' At this point she banged the table with her fist. 'Not just this country.

Internationally! Why, I've just been invited to Japan. An international seminar!'

'I'm sorry.' Maxine apologised. 'But you said ...'

Mrs Oribine sat down again. 'I know I shouldn't have done it. It was wrong. But I thought I would do it just once. To set her mind at ease. She was so troubled.' She smiled at Maxine then. 'And I could feel such sadness in your house ... and all around you, hen. I could see you were going through a trauma.'

A trauma. Maxine wasn't a hundred per cent sure what it meant, but she liked the sound of it.

'And something else. I can see it now. It's all around you like an aura. Something is happening in your life. Something scary and it's all connected with your brother.' Maxine shivered, remembering now the puzzled look that had passed over Luella's face the night of the seance. Maybe she really did have a gift. 'I just felt if I could get your mother to move on, I might be helping you too.'

'But it was like ... opening a door, and my mum won't let it shut again.'

Mrs Oribine seemed impressed by that idea. 'Yes,' she said, 'that's it. She won't let the door shut. I tried to do the right thing. I really did. I could see what you and your dad were going through. I tried to tell her that Derek wouldn't come through again. That he just wanted her to get on with her life. To look after the family she had left.' Mrs Oribine sighed. 'I hoped in time she'd come to terms with his loss. People do. And then they're ready to move on. I refused to sit with her again, you know.'

That surprised Maxine. 'But I thought she was seeing you often.'

'Not me. But she went to other mediums. They might be doing the same thing for all I know. Just trying to help her. But there are a lot of charlatans in this business. I only hope she hasn't got in tow with any of them.'

Charlatans? Luella Oribine knew some lovely words.

'However, I'm ready now to go and see your mother and explain everything, if that's what you want.'

Was that what she wanted? Would it help her mother to know it had all been a lie? Or would that knowledge only make things worse?

'Why do you think you didn't get a message from Derek?' Maxine asked after a lot of thought.

'Who knows?' Luella Oribine noticed a spot on her table and began spraying polish on it. 'Perhaps he's

145

content wherever he is. Doesn't want to come through. I did try everything.' She went on, 'I held many of your brother's belongings to try to make contact, and still nothing. Maybe if I'd had something he was wearing when he went missing –'

Maxine interrupted her excitedly. 'What difference would that make?'

Luella knocked her ash into the ashtray. 'A person's energy remains in their belongings for a long time. Sometimes it's so strong you can almost feel them beside you. But, of course, perhaps your brother had been gone for so long, all that energy had gone with him.'

Maxine put her hand in her pocket and touched the medal. 'Do you mean, if I had something Derek was wearing when he went missing ... you might be able to contact him?'

'Possibly. Why?'

Maxine drew the chain from her pocket and laid it out on the table in front of her. 'This was Derek's,' she said.

Mrs. Oribine was obviously puzzled. How much could she tell her? This woman was used to strange stories. She'd believe anything. And yet ...

'I bought this for him,' Maxine explained. 'His last birthday before he left. He never took it off.'

She let that statement hang in the air. He never took it off, so he must have been wearing it when he died. She prayed the medium wouldn't ask how she got it.

Mrs Oribine reached out for the chain. 'It's lovely,' she said. She held it in her hands, entwining it around her fingers, turning the medal to read the inscription. 'Derek Moody.' Her face creased into a frown.

'Is something wrong?' Maxine watched her closely. Mrs Oribine closed her hands around the medal and clutched it to her. As she did so, she gasped. The colour seemed to drain from her face. Her breathing became faster. Maxine stood up and approached her. It was as if Luella Oribine wasn't there any more. Her eyes glazed over. She let out a little moan and held the chain closer against her. 'Such strong feelings!' she murmured. 'Where did you get this?'

She didn't wait for an answer. Beads of sweat were appearing on her brow. 'Such pain. Such fear. No ... Terror! Running away. Someone's after him. He's so scared. I can feel his terror. He doesn't know what else to do. He has to run.' Suddenly she threw the chain from her. It clattered across the table and slid to the floor.

Maxine picked up the chain and held it in her hand, exactly as Luella Oribine had done. Nothing. She could feel nothing. It was still warm from Luella Oribine's grasp, but it was only a St Christopher medal on a golden chain.

Mrs Oribine's hands were shaking as she came to. She pulled another cigarette from her packet and lit it nervously. She didn't say a word until she'd taken one long pull. Only then did she speak, in a voice that sounded almost afraid. 'Thank goodness that didn't happen in front of your mother.' She looked at Maxine and there were tears in her eyes. She shook her head.

'Maxine, hen. What was it your brother was so terrified of?'

CHAPTER TWENTY-TWO

Cam was in when she phoned. She thanked every saint she could think of for that. She needed to talk to someone about what had happened at Luella Oribine's. She told him breathlessly and waited with impatience for his reaction. If he laughed or told her she was stupid, she'd call him every name. She'd slam the phone down. She'd scream!

But he didn't laugh. 'This is serious, Maxine. You've got to do something. Whoever is behind this could be dangerous. You have to tell the police.'

'And tell them what? The only proof I have is the word of a dotty old fortune teller.'

'Your parents have to know.'

'I tried that before, remember? Dad almost threw me out of the house.'

'You have the medal now.'

The medal. Yes, she had the medal. But how could she explain it to Dad? How could he explain it to Mum? The thought of that made her decision easy. 'You're the only one I want to know, Cam. I can't tell them.'

She listened to his long sigh of disapproval. She hated it when he acted like a big brother. 'OK, but when he contacts you again, you don't go anywhere alone. I'm going with you.'

'He won't contact me again.'

'Yes, he will. He's not going to leave it be now. He'll want to know your reaction to the medal. He'll be in touch.'

Maxine didn't want that. She wanted to throw the medal down the nearest drain and pretend none of this had ever happened.

As she replaced the receiver, she wondered why Cam always believed her so readily. He had never heard the voice on the phone. He only had her word that there was someone else in the church that day. So she had the medal. How was he to know she hadn't had the medal all along, hidden away in a drawer somewhere?

Yet he believed everything she told him. Why? He didn't even like her. He had liked her brother less. So why was he helping her?

There were two answers to that. The first, and the least likely, was that Cam really did fancy her. The second, and it sent shivers up her spine to even consider it, was that it was Cam who was behind the whole thing. He was certainly clever enough to think up such a plan.

But why? Because Derek had taunted him? No. It was silly even to think about it.

She was becoming ... what was the word ... haemorrhoid? Schizoid? Paranoid? Whatever it was, she was definitely becoming one of them.

'And where have you been today?' her father asked her as soon as he came in from work.

Maxine's face flushed guiltily. 'Where have I been? Me?'

How much did he know? Had Luella Oribine phoned him at his office and told him about Derek's medal? Surely not. She'd promised Maxine not to breathe a word. It would only distress her parents further. No. She was as dotty as a spotted dick but when she gave her word Maxine was convinced she wouldn't break it. She wouldn't have phoned Dad.

Her father sighed impatiently. 'It was a simple

enough question, Maxine. Where have you been today? What have you been up to?'

He didn't miss the guilty look on her face.

'And I'd say you've been up to something.' He just stopped himself in time from accusing her. 'Those phone calls you say you were getting. Have they stopped?'

Maybe there were such things as psychic messages. She had been thinking about them, and here he was, asking about them. 'Have you had any more?' He sounded sympathetic. 'Because if you have, I'd insist we go to the police. I won't have any crank doing that to you.'

'Do ... do you think we should?'

And if they did, perhaps all her troubles would be over.

'If you've not had any more calls, it's best forgotten. I know what you're thinking,' he said. 'Bringing the police in wouldn't help your mother at all. Bring it all back to her. Let's just forget it, shall we?'

Maxine sighed as he walked away. If she'd had any doubts before, they were completely wiped out now. Tell her parents? That was a joke. First she'd have to get them to listen.

There had been no more calls. That was what she'd told Dad. But maybe there was something in this psychic business after all. Because that very night she had another.

Mum and Dad had gone out. They hadn't told her where, leaving Mrs Templeton to babysit. Babysit! How embarrassing! It was only an excuse for the old devil to do her laundry in Mum's machine. When the phone rang, the old dear didn't even hear it.

The voice was soft and breathless, but it was the same voice she had heard in the shadows of the church.

'I'm sorry about the statue. It was an accident.'

She didn't answer him. She wasn't sure that was true.

'Now that you know I am Derek ...' He hesitated, waiting for her to verify this. Well, she would. She'd pretend she believed everything he said. 'We have to meet again. We have to talk.'

'I thought we were going to do that in church?'

'Someone was coming. I don't want anyone else to know I'm here. That's why I ran.'

'I don't understand why you just can't come home.'

'I'll tell you that when I meet you. I promise. I'll tell you everything.'

That decided her. 'OK, so where are we going to meet?'

He had obviously already thought about that, for he answered immediately. 'In the cemetery. At my grave.' She heard him catch his breath. 'Do you know how strange it is to be saying that ... at my grave?'

'The cemetery?' she asked him. 'Why the cemetery?' It seemed a morbid place for a meeting.

'Because it's the safest place,' he said softly.

CHAPTER
TWENTY-THREE

'You told him you'd meet him in the cemetery?' Cam's voice on the phone was totally incredulous.

'He said it was the safest place.'

'For him, maybe. Certainly not for you. You can't meet him there, Maxine. You should have insisted on somewhere else.'

Maxine tutted. According to smart alec Cam, everything she did was wrong. 'He wouldn't go anywhere else. I'm supposed to meet him tomorrow afternoon.'

'After school?'

'No. Not after school. During school hours. It'll be even quieter then.' The words echoed eerily in her mind.

'Yes, Maxine. Exactly. This boy, whoever he is, is dangerous. You have to tell your parents about this!'

'Will you shut up about telling my parents! I'm not telling them and that's final. And remember, you promised you wouldn't tell them either.'

At last he gave up. 'All right. But I'm going with you.'

'You're taking time off school for me?' She was really impressed. 'Goodness, Cam, are you sure you don't fancy me?'

'Hold on to the phone. I'm going to be sick,' he said.

She was almost sure he was smiling when he said that. 'Cam,' she went on after a pause. 'He sounded scared.' And he had, this boy who said he was her brother had sounded terrified.

'Good actor,' Cam said at once.

'You don't think he could be ... Derek, do you?'

'No. I don't think he could be Derek. Derek's dead and buried, Maxine. Your father identified him, remember? This isn't *Tales from the Crypt*. This is real life.'

'I know ... ' she said, 'but I was thinking of a film I saw just recently. Putting on Derek's clothes and –looking like Derek doesn't mean the dead boy was Derek.'

'Rubbish!' Cam was sure of himself. She needed that reassurance. 'Your father identified the body. Of course it was Derek. Don't build up impossible hopes, Maxine.'

156

But was that what she hoped? That it was Derek? Hadn't she always said she wanted him gone, for ever?

Her parents came home not long after her call to Cam. There was a tension between them, as if something had happened. Mum didn't say a word. She pulled off her coat and slung it across a chair in the hall. Then she went upstairs. Dad came into the living room where Maxine sat watching TV.

'Shouldn't you be doing homework?' he said, then added sarcastically, 'Or aren't you bothering with homework now?'

Maxine sighed. It was so typical. Whenever they're in a bad mood, take it out on Maxine.

'Sorry,' he said, regretting it almost immediately. 'Bad night with your mother.'

'Why? Where did you go?'

He sat down beside her. 'I took her to speak to someone. I thought it might help.'

'A psychiatrist?'

'A therapist,' he corrected. 'She's very good. But your mother ...' He ran his hands through his hair the way he did when he'd just about had enough. 'Sometimes I think she's beyond help.'

157

'Do you think it helps her getting these messages from Derek?'

'Maybe it did at first. But now it's an obsession. That's what worries me. What she really wants is the impossible. She wants Derek back.'

Maxine had it in her power to give her mother hope. Only ... it wasn't Derek. It couldn't be. Telling anyone but Cam would only make things worse.

'It was definitely Derek you identified, Dad?'

Wrong thing to say, she knew it at once. Her father went red with anger. 'For heaven's sake, Maxine! How can you say such a thing?' Her father, always the gentlest of dads, was angrier than she'd ever seen him.

She tried to think of the right way to put it to calm him down. 'I only meant ... putting on Derek's clothes doesn't mean it was Derek.'

He leapt to his feet and Maxine could see the tears starting in his eyes. 'That was the hardest thing I ever had to do in my life, Maxine. Don't you dare try to say I made a mistake! Derek was seen in that squat, wearing those clothes. Don't you think I'd know my own son?'

Maxine tried to explain. He wouldn't listen.

'Do you think this is going to help your mother?

Because it won't. Accepting his death is all that will help her now. And you too, Maxine. You'd better accept it too.'

'Accept what?' Her mother was standing in the doorway, looking small and vulnerable.

Dad swung round. 'Nothing!' he snapped. His glance at Maxine warned her to keep quiet too.

Mum stiffened. 'Something I'm not supposed to know about, obviously.'

She didn't look at him as he began to storm out of the room. 'And by the way,' he called back angrily, 'we're all going to that therapist tomorrow afternoon.'

Tomorrow afternoon! But what about her meeting with the boy who called himself Derek? Maxine immediately began to make all sorts of excuses.

Dad was determined. 'You're going, Maxine. If I have to carry you there.' Then he was gone, slamming the door behind him.

'He thinks I'm crazy,' Mum said calmly.

'Don't worry about it, Mum. He thinks I'm crazy too.'

No amount of persuasion next morning at breakfast would make him change his mind. Important classes

Maxine just couldn't afford to miss, life-changing studies that she mustn't take time from. Nothing. She was going and that was that.

'Miss Ross will have you at the school gate at lunchtime. I'll be there to pick you up. Right?'

He even waited to drive her to school, just to make sure she went. She had no idea how she was going to get out of this one.

She didn't find Cam until the break to tell him the news. His expression didn't change. Did nothing ever upset this guy? 'I think I still might go,' he said.

'But it'll be dangerous.'

'Ah, you mean without you there to protect me. All six and a half stone of you.'

'I don't see the point of you going on your own.'

Cam began to explain, very slowly, as if she was an idiot. He could be quite offensive at times. 'He doesn't know you've told me any of this. I'll go up there, as if I'm visiting a grave. I want to see him for myself.'

'He'll be hiding,' she told him.

'But I'll be looking for him.'

She had to give in. She wasn't going to be able to go and that was the end of it. 'Oh, all right then, but you'd better be careful.'

160

He smiled at her. It occurred to her then that she was good for Cam. He'd never smiled so much in his life. This smile, however, was taking the mickey. 'Ah, Maxine, I didn't know you cared.'

He said it at exactly the wrong time. Miss Ross was suddenly there, seeing the smile, hearing the words. 'Quite a little romance going on here, is there?'

Cam almost exploded. Before he could say a word, Maxine broke in with a mischievous grin. 'Do you think we're suited, Miss?'

Miss Ross was nothing if not candid. 'I wouldn't have thought so. I believe that really smart girl in third year was more Cam's type. And I know she likes him.'

Cam's eyes lit up. 'You mean that redhead?'

Miss Ross nodded.

'And she likes me?' His smile, Maxine thought, had turned into a stupid grin.

'But I can see what Maxine's got too,' Miss Ross went on. 'It's that sense of humour, isn't it?'

Cam began to look ill. 'I better get to my class.'

Suddenly, Maxine remembered she wouldn't see him now until after ... after what? She hardly dared to think about it. She wanted to tell him again to be careful, not take any stupid chances. She was afraid for him, but she could say nothing. Miss Ross was there.

'Cam?' she called after him and he turned round. 'I'll see you later?'

Cam glanced at Miss Ross. He didn't want her to think there was anything going on between them, yet this conversation was practically proving it. He looked even sicker as he answered her. 'I'll come over tonight, OK?'

Then he hurried off down the corridor to his next class.

'It's good to see you looking so happy, Maxine,' Miss Ross said. 'Your dad's been on the phone about this meeting he's arranged.'

'I don't want to go, Miss. Couldn't you tell him I don't have to? I can't miss school.'

'I think it's an excellent idea. Family therapy. This has affected all of you. I really think this might be the answer, Maxine.'

But not today of all days, she wanted to scream. Today was too important.

Suddenly Miss Ross's voice rang out angrily, making Maxine jump. 'What are you doing here, Sweeney!' It wasn't a question. It was a reproof. Maxine gulped as Sweeney appeared from the doorway behind her.

'Goin' to my next class, Miss,' he said in his gruff voice.

'Well, get going then. Right now!'

He glanced at Maxine as he brushed past her. There was a malicious smile in those eyes, she thought. She shivered. How long had Sweeney been hiding in there ... and how much had he heard?

CHAPTER TWENTY-FOUR

'You could at least be polite. The doctor is trying to help us.'

Both Maxine and her mum were sitting glumly outside Dr Rice's office. Her father was holding a tight rein on his anger. But Maxine didn't want to be there. Neither did her mother. So why did they have to look as if they were enjoying it? Her mother seemed to have the same thought.

'This was your idea,' Mum snapped. 'Not ours. We're going along with it. What more do you want?'

Dad was ready to give her an answer when the door opened and Dr Rice came out.

She was much younger than Maxine had expected. She had a wide smile and white, even teeth. Her shiny, black hair was cut into a neat, silky bob. She took off her gold-rimmed glasses to greet them.

'Mr Moody. Mrs Moody. Good of you to come back.'
She held out her hand. 'And you must be Maxine.'

Maxine had been prepared not to like her. Determined, even. But it was hard not to warm to that smile.

'Come into my office,' she said. 'You had no problems getting time off school?'

Glad to be rid of me, probably, she almost said. Instead she simply answered, 'No.'

'I really did think it was important for me to see you all together.' She ushered them into three comfortable chairs beside her own. Maxine looked around for a couch. Didn't they always have couches? Dr Rice followed her eyes and smiled again. 'No, Maxine. No couch. Not even a desk. This is very informal. I just want you to talk.'

'I don't know why you needed me here again,' Mum said with a little edge to her voice. 'I said everything I wanted to say last night.'

'I know that. But Maxine wasn't here last night. And if you want to get through this I think Maxine has to be involved.'

They were actually getting her involved at last? This was amazing. Maxine started to be interested.

'I am getting through it!' Mum snapped the words

out. 'In my own way.' She threw a chilling look at Dad. 'If some people would just let me be.'

'Going to a seance every day to contact your dead son is not getting through it, Gill!'

Dr Rice quietened them both before it became a full-scale war. She looked at Maxine. 'Why don't we all listen to what Maxine has to say? Maxine, what do you think about all this?'

She was taken aback. Too surprised to say anything for a moment. No one had ever asked her that before. She was always too young. Pushed into another room while it was discussed. Kept out of every discovery, every piece of news. Now both her mum and dad were looking at her, waiting for her answer.

Well, if someone was going to listen at last ... she was going to talk!

Her voice trembled as she began. She talked about the day Derek had gone. How she felt as the days passed and there was no word of him. And then the weeks, and the months. Watching the pain of her parents as they tried everything to trace him. Finally, she talked about finding out that Derek was dead.

'I know how much it hurt Mum and Dad when Derek went away. I know how terrible it must have been to

find out he was dead. But what I don't understand is ...'
She drew in a deep breath, determined not to cry. She
had to say it all, now that she had started. 'Why did that
stop them loving me?'

Her father gasped. Her mother clutched at his hand.
Dr Rice gestured to them to be quiet. 'What makes you
think they stopped loving you, Maxine?'

'I was pushed out. They looked for Derek and I was
sent to stay with anyone who would have me. They
talked about Derek. He was all they thought about.
Everything was Derek. No matter what I did, they
didn't notice I was there. Derek was all they cared
about. We've never really known why Derek ran away.
But I've always had the feeling ... they think it was my
fault.'

'Oh no, Maxine!' Mum was beginning to cry, but Dr
Rice still wouldn't let her speak.

'Go on, Maxine,' she urged.

'I used to wish Derek was dead!' Now Maxine could
feel the tears spilling over. 'I know that's a terrible thing
to say. But I thought if he was dead, they'd start to care
about me again. And then he was, and I thought that
was all my fault too. And then I realised it didn't matter
anyway, because even though he was dead, he was still

all they cared about, all they talked about. Derek. Derek. Derek!'

'Oh no, Maxine! You couldn't be more wrong. My poor wee girl!' Her father leaned across to her and pulled her close.

'Can I say something now?' Her mother's voice was soft, yet somehow stronger than Maxine had heard it in months. She was holding her tears in check.

'You think we blamed you? But I've always thought it was my fault. He wanted to talk to me that morning. He had something he had to tell me. I jumped down his throat, sure he'd got into more trouble at school. Done something else wrong. I gave him such a row. He'd been behaving so badly for so long. He started yelling. He couldn't talk to me, he said. I never listened. I realise now that was probably true. And I've always wondered what it was he wanted to tell me. And if I'd listened ... would he have run away?'

'I'm just as guilty,' Dad said quietly. 'Not listening, when he needed to talk. All that time he was being bullied I felt I did nothing to help. I felt so useless. Going up to the school didn't seem to do any good at all. So I just told him to fight back ... and then when he did, I was angry. Felt he'd become a bully himself. Now, I think maybe he was trying to get our attention, just the way you did, Maxine. And I'm so afraid I'm making the same mistakes with you ... and I'd die if you ever left us. Do you realise that, Maxine? I don't think I could go on if you left too.'

Mum buried her face in her hands. 'Never think we don't love you. If anything were to happen to you ...' She began to sob.

Dad went on, his voice soft. 'I know Derek took over our lives, Maxine. It was the not knowing was the worst. Not knowing why he'd left. Where he was. If he was safe or in danger. And I was watching your mum, she was falling apart with the worry of it. Her life was finding Derek, so I had to be with her.' He stopped for a moment. Then he continued in an even softer voice. 'I've never confessed this to anyone. But when we heard Derek was dead ... I was relieved. I'm so ashamed to say that. Relieved.'

Her mum let out a sob then, but she said nothing. Maxine almost cried too. Relieved. Her dad had felt the same as she did, and she hadn't known.

'I thought at last things could get back to normal. We knew the worst.' Dad gripped his wife's hand in his, hugged Maxine close to him. 'But it didn't get back to normal. It only seemed to make things worse. And we were so wrapped up in ourselves, we forgot the most important person. You, Maxine.'

They loved her. Everything was going to be all right. Mum was going to be all right. Maxine knew it would take time, but they would get there. As long as she knew they really did love her. And suddenly, like a great dark cloud hiding the sun, she remembered the boy in the cemetery. If only she could tell them now about him! About all the things that had been happening to her. But if today was a new beginning for them, she knew she could never tell them that. Mum might never get over it. She wasn't going to take that risk. Never.

Mum smiled through her tears. 'We're all going to try harder, aren't we?' she said. 'A day at a time?'

They had a chance. If it wasn't for the boy in the cemetery. Whoever he was, he could ruin everything. Her fears must have shown on her face, for Dr Rice asked her, 'Are you feeling OK, Maxine?'

'There's something she's not telling us.' Her father saw that right away. 'Maxine, what is it? Now's the time to be honest with each other.'

But what could she tell them? That someone was pretending to be Derek, and that she was meant to be meeting him today? She glanced at the clock on the wall. She *had* to meet him. Tell him to get out of their lives for ever. She wanted it to be finished. Finished for good. She might just make it to the cemetery in time.

'I ... have to go!' she said, jumping from her chair. 'I promised I'd meet Cam.'

There was alarm in her mother's face. Maxine kissed her quickly and smiled. 'I'm so happy, Mum. And I'll be home soon, I promise. And then everything will be fine.'

And then she was off, with her father calling after her.

Mum would be fine. She knew that now. She would begin to accept Derek's death.

As long as she never heard anything of this business.

Well, she never would. Maxine would make sure of it. It was over. She headed for the cemetery and Cam. Together they would confront this boy. Threaten him with the police, with anything, get him to leave and never come back. She might still just be in time to catch them together.

The great, green gates of the cemetery lay open. Twilight was beginning to descend on an already dark day.

This was it. Maxine took a deep breath and hurried inside.

CHAPTER TWENTY-FIVE

Had there ever been a darker, more gloomy afternoon? The black clouds hung heavy, almost touching the tops of the monkey-puzzle trees, and an eerie mist weaved its way through the branches. Darkness was already falling.

Maxine hurried up the long, narrow paths that led to Derek's grave, listening intently for the least sound. What would she find? Anything? All she knew was that she wanted it finished. Now, when she could see light at the end of the tunnel, she wanted nothing more of this 'Derek'. Derek was dead.

She heard a faint cry in the distance and stopped. The hooting of a bird? But no, it was something else. There it was again. And this time she recognised it. A cry of pain. Someone was being hurt. She began to run.

She should never have let Cam come up here on his own. Whoever was doing this was wicked, wicked enough to do anything. The trees were thicker here as she moved deeper into the cemetery and the afternoon grew even darker.

She turned onto the path where Derek's grave was and gasped at what she saw.

Cam. And he was being held down and kicked by Sweeney and two of his cronies, Stew and McCabe. Cam was already bruised and bleeding. His shirt was torn, his arm twisted painfully up his back.

So, after all, it had been Sweeney all the time. Nasty, vengeful Sweeney playing his tricks on her. Hadn't she suspected it all the time? She'd always known deep down he was involved. No one else could be that cruel.

'I'll show you a karate kick, pal!' Sweeney sniggered and lifted his foot to strike at Cam's side. Cam tensed ready for the blow.

Maxine screamed, and the kick didn't come. Instead, Sweeney turned quickly and saw her. His snigger became a grin. 'It's wee Moody, come to your rescue, China boy.'

'You let him go, moron!' Maxine yelled at him.

'Maxine, get out of here! Run!' Cam could hardly get his breath, it had been kicked out of him.

Sweeney found her threat funny. 'The size of you

telling me what to do? Going to do something about it, titch?'

She made a run at him. 'If I've got to!'

She took him by surprise. He stumbled back and almost fell. Cam took the opportunity to roll away from him, but he was grabbed and kept down by the other two, Stew and McCabe.

'Keep a hold of him!' Sweeney ordered, getting his balance again. Angry now, angry that she had almost made him fall, he grabbed her by the hair and yanked.

Maxine let out another yell.

'At least you've got some spirit, hen. Not like that wimp of a brother of yours.'

She struggled to free herself, but it was no good. 'Don't you call my brother a wimp! He was better than you any day!'

She kicked out then furiously and connected with his shins. He threw her from him and she fell.

'Run, Maxine!' Cam yelled.

But Maxine didn't get the chance. As she tried to get to her feet, Sweeney pushed her down again. 'I think it's time you knew about that brother of yours.' He spat out the words, and Maxine shrank back. 'You want to know why he really ran away? 'Cause of me!' He said it as if he'd done something wonderful. 'I hated that wee wimp. Always getting his mummy and daddy up to see the headmaster.' Sweeney gave a shrug. 'So what! I'd be suspended, but see, when I'd come back ...' His laugh then was full of maliciousness. 'I'd make his life even more of a misery. It was so funny! He even thought if he was as tough as me, starting picking on people, I'd leave him alone. Some hope! He was never good at it.' Sweeney was enjoying taunting her, standing there almost on Derek's grave.

'I know he wasn't. He was better than you! He had too many brains to be a bully,' she screamed at him, and jumped to her feet.

'I didn't stop giving him hassle. I think he realised then, the wimp, that I don't give up until I'm finished with somebody. I wasn't finished with your brother, not by a long way.'

Now Maxine couldn't have run if she'd wanted to. She had to hear this out.

'The day before he ran away, I told him I had "something really special" lined up for him. Next day, when he came into the school, he was for it. And it would be something he wouldn't forget. So ... what does he do? The wimp's too scared to even come to school the next day. He runs. And he's never seen again.' Sweeney's laugh seemed to echo up into the trees. 'He ran because of me! I scared the living daylights out of him!'

So that was what Derek had wanted to tell his mother. What he had needed to talk about, and no one – *no one!* – had listened. Oh, Derek! In that moment, she was apologising. I'm so sorry, Derek.

'I'll tell everybody!' she yelled at him. 'You're evil!'

'Oh, come on, wee Maxine. I've been at this since I came into school. Remember?' He put on a pitiful voice. 'I'm a deprived child. They have to make allowances for me.' Sweeney continued, 'I'm still here ... but your wimp of a brother isn't. He's ...' He pointed down, under the earth. 'He's down there.' And then he was laughing again.

Maxine was almost crying. 'It's been you all along! Pretending he'd come back. Frightening me! I might have known! Pig!'

She screamed at him and ran again to where he stood. But this time he gripped her by the shoulders and spoke so close to her face that she could feel his spit splash against her cheeks.

'You've got more spirit than your brother, hen. But I'll soon knock that out of you. Because I've picked you as the next one. And see, from now on ... I'm going to make your life a misery as well. Day in and day out.'

She saw it all then. This was what he had done to Derek. Day in and day out, fear, fear of going to school. So he didn't go. Not getting anyone to listen, or when they did, Sweeney was only reprimanded or suspended. And then he would be back at school, and the terrorising would begin again. Only worse. Until finally, Sweeney had planned 'something special' just for Derek. Her brother's imagination would have made that 'something special' so much worse. How he must have felt that last night, knowing that school next day was going to bring the worst kind of hell! Thinking of how to escape to get away. Feeling everyone had deserted him already. He'd tried to talk to his mother and she had pushed him aside. Not wanting to listen. No one had wanted to listen or help.

No wonder he had run away, Maxine thought. She would have done.

And now Sweeney had chosen Maxine as his next victim. Now, when things could be better for her mum and dad and the family, she saw her life stretch ahead of her filled with fear. Fear of Sweeney.

Sweeney was laughing now. Watching her reaction as

if he could read her mind. 'Scary, eh?' he sniggered.

'I won't let you!' she screamed. 'I won't let you ruin my life like you did my brother's!'

'You're not going to have any choice,' Sweeney said maliciously.

'Ssssweeeney ...'

Sweeney swung round. 'What was that?'

Maxine had heard it too, but it was only a rustle in the trees, the wind whistling softly, eerily through the undergrowth.

'SSssswe-eeney ...'

And this time, no mistake, a soft, silky, ghostly voice coming from nowhere.

Sweeney swung round again. His eyes were darting everywhere. 'Who's that? Who's there?'

'It's me ... Ssssweeney ... Derek ... and I've come to get you ...'

CHAPTER TWENTY-SIX

Maxine began to shiver. The hairs on the back of her neck rose. Even Cam was silent. She could hear Sweeney's quick breathing.

'Ssssweeeeeney ... Sssswee-eney.' An eerie whispered call.

'Who's that?' he demanded.

'You woke me up, Ssssweeney.' The name was spoken like the hiss of a cobra.

'Whoever you are, I'll make you sorry.' Sweeney's voice was full of bravado, but it trembled all the same.

The cemetery grew even darker. The wind rustled and a twig cracked somewhere nearby.

Sweeney swirled round at the sound. 'I'll get you for this!'

'No, Ssssweeney. I've come to get you. It's lonely in

my grave without you, Ssssweeney. Come and join me ...'

'Who the hell is that, Sweeney?' Stew shouted. He was shaking, looking all around him, looking for something human, something alive.

'It sounded like ...' McCabe didn't want to finish. Couldn't believe it.

'It sounded like Derek,' Maxine finished for him, her voice flat.

And it did, the voice on the phone, the murmured whisper in the church. A ghost after all ... yet she wasn't afraid now. Derek wouldn't hurt her.

'I told you he'd come back one day and get you, Sweeney,' she told him.

'Here I am, Sssweeney ... here. Can't you feel me?'

Stew suddenly let go of Cam. 'I'm out of here, Sweeney. It's you he wants.'

And he was off, running, looking after him, terrified that whatever it was would stop his escape.

'Wait for me!' And McCabe was sprinting after him.

'Now, Ssssweeney ... it's just you and me ...'

Sweeney jumped around. The voice now came from somewhere behind him. 'You can't ever get away from me now, Ssssweeney ...'

Sweeeney yelled at the top of his voice, 'Where the hell are you? Come out and fight like a man!'

The laugh that came then was mingled with the wind. It might have been the wind. 'You've never fought like a man in your life. Now you're mine, for eternity, in hell, Ssssweeney. And I've got ... something special ... lined up for you.'

Sweeney let out a yell. The words he'd used to terrify Derek came back to haunt him. 'Something special' held a new terror now.

Sweeney jumped back, lost his footing and tumbled onto Derek's grave. He lay there, too terrified to move, glancing in fear all around him. Not knowing which way to look, which way to turn.

'You're coming with me, Ssssweeney ... I'm reaching up for you. Can you feel me? Any second now my hand will come *thrusting through the earth*!' The voice rose and Sweeney screamed. 'You're mine, SSSSSweeney ... Come to me!'

Still Sweeney screamed. He believed it. He looked all around the grave, waiting for Derek's hand to come pushing up through the earth, to grab him and drag him down, down, down beside Derek. Even Maxine imagined it: the hand rising, fingers spaced wide, clutching on to a terrified Sweeney and pulling him down to hell, where he belonged.

Sweeney couldn't move. He was too terrified to move.

'I'm sorry. I'm sorry! I won't touch your sister. I promise.'

Silence was his answer. And the cemetery grew darker.

The voice when it came was softer and more ghostly than ever. 'I'm taking you anyway, Ssssweeney.'

The clouds darkened, the low-hanging branches of the trees shifted in the wind and the name DEREK MOODY seemed to move with the shadows on the gravestone. Sweeney saw it too. His voice rose in terror. 'I won't touch her!' he screamed, almost in tears now. 'I won't ever touch anybody. EVER!'

He rolled off the grave and jumped to his feet. Maxine had never seen anyone so terrified, and yet she felt nothing. No sympathy. Sweeney had terrified too many others in his time. Maybe now he never would again.

He was in a panic, brushing imaginary fingers from his trousers, his jacket. His eyes were darting all round him. He started to back away, his eyes never leaving the trees and thick bushes that surrounded the graves.

It was as if he had forgotten that Maxine and Cam were still there. There was only himself ... and whatever belonged to the weird, disembodied voice in the gloomy cemetery.

He took one step back and then another.

'Watch every dark corner, Ssssweeney ... I'll be there ... waiting ...'

And breathlessly, Sweeney ran, tripping and jumping at every movement, at every sound. Clawing in terror at the overhanging branches brushing against his face. He ran in fear, until he was swallowed up in the darkness of the cemetery.

Maxine held her breath until he was gone. Gone completely. She looked at Cam. He was bruised and his trousers were torn, his tie twisted round his neck. He was looking at her too. Then both of them turned their eyes to the trees.

At first Maxine could see nothing. Except the branches dancing and shifting. And then she caught her breath. A movement. A shadowy figure, a face. The face she'd seen in the trees that day so long ago.

The face of her brother.

This time he stepped out of the shadows. He was thin and pale. He didn't look real. He said nothing at first.

He didn't even smile. He stood beside the gravestone.

DEREK MOODY
BELOVED SON

And then, in a soft trembling voice, he whispered, 'It's me, Maxie. It's Derek. I want to come home.'

CHAPTER
TWENTY-SEVEN

Derek became something of a media star, interviewed on radio and television. There were even columns written about him in national papers. His whole story was told. Of why he ran away, of how he survived on the streets and in squats, and how just seeing his death announced in one of the papers had been the spur that had made him come back. He'd wanted to see his family so much. To let them know he was still alive. He'd followed them, Maxine especially, always in the shadows, waiting for his opportunity to talk to her. But he would never have come back while Sweeney was around. He would never go back to that. 'It would all start all over again,' he had told Maxine. Now she knew what he had meant.

Derek had lived in the old mausoleums in the cemetery during those weeks, moving from one to another. He knew them all well and had never once been frightened there. There were too many real things to be afraid of, he had told reporters. He was even invited on to one of those morning chat shows to talk about bullying and tell of how many of the young people he had met when he was on the run had left home, just like him, because of the nightmares they were living at school.

Sweeney never quite got over the shock of that day. He had been terrified, right there in front of little Maxine and the Chinese boy he hated, terrified and humiliated. At last something was done about Sweeney. He was expelled, and Cam's father made sure he was charged with the assault on his son. Sweeney was out of the school, and the school breathed a sigh of relief.

Maxine didn't care. She hated him. She could never hate anyone as much as she hated Sweeney ... and yet. Try as she might, the thought kept coming to her. Why had Sweeney been so bad, so evil? She had been bad for a long time, because she was hurting so much. And Derek too had changed from the perfect son to a boy no one had particularly liked because he had tried to make Sweeney like him. Did Sweeney have a problem too? She wanted to hate him. She did hate him. And yet (why did these thoughts keep invading her mind?) Sweeney had a family who thought being cruel and vicious made you a man. She had something Sweeney would never have, a family who cared about her, who wanted her to be the best she could be. Not the worst.

Derek became something of a heart-throb. There was a mystery now to Derek, the boy who had come back from the dead. Maxine had even seen his photo pinned up in the prefects' common room. Yuck!

All this attention, in Maxine's opinion, had only turned his head. He'd be selling his autograph soon, she was sure of it.

She watched him one night a few weeks later, lying along the sofa and popping popcorn into his big mouth. 'What are you looking at?' he asked her.

'Oh, nothing,' she answered, flicking through a magazine. 'You just look so much like a creature I saw on *The X Files* the other night.'

'You can't sit here with us,' he said.

'Who's us?' she asked, although she had a feeling she already knew.

'Cam's coming over. We're going to watch a video.'

'He doesn't even like you. He told me. And you don't like him. You never did.' She couldn't understand how suddenly they had become such close friends.

Derek studied his popcorn. 'It's amazing how much more likeable he's become since I came back.'

Cam never came to see her now. He and Derek were inseparable. Now she had two of them to contend with. 'Anyway, it's my house too. I can watch the video with you.'

The doorbell rang just then. 'That'll be Cam. And there is no way you are watching a video with us.'

Maxine stood up. 'I'll ask Mum. She'll let me.'

Mum came into the hallway just as Derek opened the door to Cam. She was trying to fix on one of her earrings. She looked so different now. The glow had come back into her cheeks, the brightness to her eyes.

Maxine would always remember that moment when she and Cam had brought Derek back to her. She had been sitting by the fire, and she had turned as Maxine entered, and smiled her pale smile. And then Maxine had stood aside without a word. What words were there to say? How could she tell her? She had simply stepped aside, and Derek was there. And the strange thing was, her mother hadn't screamed with disbelief. She hadn't fainted. Tears had begun to spill down her cheeks and she had opened her arms to him, and Derek had run to her. Her beloved son had come back. She had never given up hope. She had always believed that he would. Maybe her mother was as psychic as Luella Oribine.

'Derek,' she was saying now. 'I don't see why Maxine can't watch the video with you.' Then she disappeared back into the kitchen.

Derek looked at Cam. 'We're not letting her. Are we, Cam?'

'For all you know, Derek Moody, Cam might be here to see me.'

That struck both of them as funny.

'Well, maybe if I'd had my brain removed,' Cam said.

'And your eyes.' This was Derek. 'Go on, Cam. Give her a kiss. Who knows, she might turn into a beautiful princess.' By this time they were almost doubled up with their own wit. 'I mean, that's what usually happens when you kiss a frog.'

Maxine let out a yell and ran at them both. Derek held her at arm's length while she punched thin air.

Mum suddenly zoomed from the kitchen. 'Will you two behave!'

They both stopped guiltily. They had tried, when Derek had first returned, to be friends. It was easy then. She was so happy to have him back. So happy just to see

189

the glow of joy on her mother's face, to see the smile back on her father's. It didn't last, though. They were brother and sister, and there was no point in going against nature. They weren't meant to get on.

The bitterness had gone, though. And that would never come back.

Mum was pulling on her coat. 'You can all come with me, then.'

'Where are you going?'

'To church. I'm going to Saturday evening mass.'

And there, Maxine knew, she would put up a special candle as she always did now, for the boy who had been buried in Derek's grave.

'Some mother, somewhere,' she had said, 'is going through what I went through. She may never know what became of her son. It's up to us not to forget him, for her sake.'

She looked around them all now. 'Well, what's it to be? Does Maxine watch the video with you? Or do you all come to church with Dad and me?'

Dad lifted the car keys from the hall table and threw them in the air, laughing. 'Well, Gill, that soon shut them up.'

Her dad was so different now too. For a while Maxine

had wondered how he could possibly have identified another boy as his own son. His explanation made her realise that he had felt exactly the same as she did. 'I suppose in a way, I wanted it to be Derek,' he had told her. 'If Derek was dead, maybe your mother would accept that. There would be a funeral. It would be finished. Maybe everything would get back to normal. And I was so sure it *was* Derek. The same size, the same build, and other people in the squat had seen him in those clothes. Of course, I know now the boy they saw wasn't Derek at all. It was the other boy, but at the time I felt it just had to be Derek.'

'Looks as if we're stuck with her, Cam.' Derek gave in with a grin.

'Yippee!' Maxine yelled, jumping in the air.

'Your sister's not right in the head. You know that, don't you, Derek?' Cam said.

'It runs in the family,' Maxine told him, determined to get the last word.

The family, she thought. What a lovely word! Maxine's favourite.

Family.

Derek, her brother, the prodigal son, back in the fold.

The family, together again.

National Missing Persons Helpline is a
charity (Reg No 1020419) that tries to
contact missing people and offers advice
and support for their families as they
wait for news. They run a Helpline
especially for young people who have
run away, enabling them to send a message
to their family or carer and to receive
advice and help:

MESSAGE HOME HELPLINE 0800 700 740